"It's been a long time, Rose. How are you?"

How are you? After all they'd been through and all that had happened between them... What kind of question was that? This man had torn her world apart and now he wanted to make small talk? Her insides rolled. "Fine," she blurted. "Mule Hollow is a great place." How was she chatting when she wanted to throw up? Pass out. Run.

"That's what I hear," he said, his gaze searching hers. "Here, do you want me to take those for you?"

"No!" she exclaimed, and jerked away. Experiencing his touch again was the last thing she wanted. She was amazed she didn't drop her packages. More amazed she didn't throw them at him.

"I—I really need to be going. I have to get to work. But I'm sure we'll see each other again. This is a small town."

Too small for the both of them, she thought, angling past him.

"That's what I'm counting on."

Books by Debra Clopton

Love Inspired

*The Trouble with Lacy Brown
*And Baby Makes Five
*No Place Like Home
*Dream a Little Dream
*Meeting Her Match
*Operation: Married by Christmas
*Next Door Daddy
*Her Baby Dreams
*The Cowboy Takes a Bride
*Texas Ranger Dad

*Mule Hollow

DEBRA CLOPTON

was a 2004 Golden Heart finalist in the inspirational category, a 2006 Inspirational Readers' Choice Award winner, a 2007 Golden Quill Award winner and a finalist for the 2007 American Christian Fiction Writers Book of the Year Award. She praises the Lord each time someone votes for one of her books, and takes it as an affirmation that she is exactly where God wants her to be.

Debra is a hopeless romantic and loves to create stories with lively heroines and the strong heroes who fall in love with them. But most importantly she loves showing her characters living their faith, seeking God's will in their lives one day at a time. Her goal is to give her readers an entertaining story that will make them smile, hopefully laugh and always feel God's goodness as they read her books. She has found the perfect home for her stories writing for the Love Inspired line and still has to pinch herself just to see if she really is awake and living her dream.

When she isn't writing she enjoys taking road trips, reading and spending time with her two sons, Chase and Kris. She loves hearing from readers and can be reached through her Web site, www.debraclopton.com, or P.O. Box 1125, Madisonville, Texas 77864.

Texas Ranger Dad
Debra Clopton

Steeple Hill®

Published by Steeple Hill Books™

STEEPLE HILL BOOKS

Steeple
Hill®

Recycling programs
for this product may
not exist in your area.

ISBN-13: 978-0-373-87524-5
ISBN-10:   0-373-87524-X

TEXAS RANGER DAD

Copyright © 2009 by Debra Clopton

www.SteepleHill.com

Printed in U.S.A.

For you who revere my name, the sun of righteousness will rise with healing in its wings.

—*Malachi* 4:2

To my lifelong buddies and best friends in all the world, Debra Drake and Lisa Webb—the fun and laughter we've shared through the years is the inspiration that fuels my stories today! God truly blessed me with your friendship.

Chapter One

Zane Cantrell was looking for a woman. And not just any woman.

As a Texas Ranger, he'd made a career of either tracking or protecting men, women and sometimes even children. But this time it was different. This time it was personal.

His gut twisted and his jaw tightened. He wasn't a Ranger anymore; still, following her to this small town of Mule Hollow had been the easy part.

Facing her…that was where the hard part would begin.

"Zane Cantrell?"

Hearing his name, Zane turned just in time to see a giant of a man emerge from Sam's Diner. A broad smile spread across the man's chiseled features. Given the gold star pinned over his heart and the fact that only one person knew he'd been due to arrive in town late last night, Zane took this to be Sheriff Brady Cannon.

When Zane had called inquiring about a job, the sheriff had surprised him by hiring him as deputy within minutes. Of course he'd been officially checked out and no doubt the background check had revealed his story—at least most of it. The sheriff didn't know about Rose. Didn't know that Zane had more reasons than just a bum leg to take early retirement.

"Sheriff Cannon?" Zane said, extending his hand for a brisk shake.

"Glad you made it. I see you found the apartment all right."

A funny statement, since there were only two intersecting streets. Zane's mood eased with a feeling of finding a kindred spirit in his new boss. "I didn't have too much trouble," he said.

"It's not exactly Corpus, is it?"

One side of Zane's mouth lifted. "Not by a long shot."

Only seven hours separated the two places, but they seemed worlds apart. However, his leg injury required frequent stops to walk and stretch the recovering tendons. Because of that it had taken him eleven hours. He'd arrived in town shortly after ten, long after the streets had been rolled up. In Corpus, the nightlife would have just been getting started. He doubted the police here had much going on at any time of the day.

"Thanks for locating the apartment for me. You didn't have to do that, but I appreciate it." He glanced behind him at his new home over Mule Hollow's only real estate office. That it had twenty steep steps was a painful blessing Zane welcomed. Every step would help him heal more quickly.

"I'm the one who should be thanking you," Brady was quick to counter. "Having a man with your credentials call up out of the blue looking for a job, *especially* when I'm in need of help—it goes without saying that

I'm pleased." He chuckled. "And my wife insists you're a godsend. Come on, let's go around the corner to the office."

A godsend. Zane could only pray that God was directing his steps here.

Rose Vincent lived here.

And that was Zane's only reason for coming. Plain and simple.

Falling into step with his new boss, he surveyed the tiny town in the daylight. "I don't believe I've ever seen such a colorful place." Each building along Main Street was painted a different color. The feed store was yellow, the diner grass-green and across the street was a pink hair salon among a row of equally bright buildings. When he'd walked down the stairs that morning and seen the town in the light of day for the first time, he'd been startled. But he'd adjusted, liking the idea of Rose living in a place that looked so…happy. Especially after learning about the years she'd had between then and now. The time she and her son had spent in hiding, struggling and alone, because he'd failed her. It was a small comfort to know she'd found this place. He owed this town a debt of gratitude.

Brady's expression warmed. "The people are just as colorful. You won't find a better group of folks. The pace around here is pretty slow, but with all the festivals and weekend traffic we've started attracting, it can get wild sometimes. Keeps me busy and me and my wife have got a baby on the way so I really need the extra help."

"I'm glad to be of help," he said, and knew he meant it.

"So how's the leg?" Brady asked.

They turned the corner at the end of town, their

boots clicking on the plank sidewalk. Though he could usually hide the weakness, the sound of his boots hitting the wooden planks accentuated the limp. "It's coming along." He'd been up front about his healing process from the injury that had almost killed him. He'd already assured Brady before taking the job that he was on the road to a full recovery. That was all the talking he planned to do. However, that wasn't what had Zane's answer stuck in his throat as they approached the sheriff's office. It was the color of the law enforcement headquarters—chocolate brown with… It couldn't be.

Rose trim on a sheriff's office just wasn't right. Then again, maybe it was red and he simply had Rose on his mind. The thought of being this close to her again after all these years had his attention distracted beyond repair. Almost as much as Zane feared their ability to reconcile the past would be.

Brady glanced over his shoulder and chuckled. "You'll get used to it. The ladies came up with the color scheme."

"That's a relief," Zane said, forcing a grin as he followed Brady inside the office. Paint was the last thing he was going to have to get used to in this new life. But if he could make things right by Rose then he'd be satisfied. It was a lot to ask of her. During his recovery, though, he'd realized he had to try. God had given him time to make things right…God had given him a second chance and he was taking it.

"So everything is here?" Rose Vincent asked, eyeing the packages spread out across the counter of Pete's Feed and Seed.

"Goggles. Two pair. Just like you wanted," the

robust store owner said, pulling them out of the stack. "Two thick work shirts. One for you and one for Max. Leather work gloves, bandanas and a pair of size-seven boots."

It was all here. "I just feel giddy, Pete. This is so thrilling. Not to mention I now own a pair of cowboy boots!"

Pete shook his head and grinned. "Greenhorns— Oh, I almost forgot." He pulled two small canisters from the shelf behind him and set them on the counter. "You don't want to forget your blowtorches."

Rose laughed. She couldn't help it. "Max cannot wait to get his hands on those. Thanks so much for showing him how to use them correctly."

"It's a guy thing and he didn't need much teaching. Y'all are gonna do real good with this venture, Rose."

She took a deep breath and started stacking the boxes. Her heart was bursting with emotions she couldn't put into words. If Pete only knew what it had taken for her to get to this point in her life. A life that hadn't turned out anything like she'd envisioned it. And yet despite everything that had happened to her, she'd come to realize that she was finally happy.

More important, Max was happy. Her son was so excited about the new business they were starting together…even if it was selling jelly. The idea made her smile. Her grandmother's wonderful jelly recipe was the perfect foundation with which to build their new future. God rest her soul; she'd always wanted the best for Rose.

Her heartstrings tugged as always when she thought of her grandmother. Oh, how she missed her. "I'm going to bring you my first jar of prickly pear jelly."

Pete rubbed his belly. "I can hardly wait. Let me carry these packages out to your car for you."

"Oh, no, you don't," she said. "I can get this. You have better things to do and I have two capable arms." She proved it by scooping the stack of boxes into them.

"I don't feel right about you carryin' all that," Pete grumbled, leaning across the counter to balance the top boxes as they teetered.

"That's because your momma raised you right. But really, I've got this. You have feed orders waiting to be filled, so go on and take care of that and stop worrying about me."

He didn't look convinced, but didn't push the issue as Rose headed for the door. She'd learned a man with manners was a wonderful thing, but she wasn't one to get used to such things. She glanced back to reassure him. "You have a great day," she called. Her excitement about the boxes in her arms had her quickening her steps toward the door. Max was waiting at home, eager to start their first fruit harvest.

It was amazing, through years of bitter disillusionment, betrayal and a broken heart God had led her and Max here—to this new life they were starting today. She'd never felt so exhilarated or optimistic about her life. She was practically singing as she stepped out into the bright sunshiny day.

And straight into a wall of a man!

"Whoa, there," he rumbled from behind the grass separating them.

Rose froze. *That voice!*

Shock washed over her—if it hadn't been for his strong hands holding her up, her knees might have buckled beneath her. Dazed, she looked over the packages into the eyes of a two-legged skunk.

"Rose."

Her name coming from Zane Cantrell's lips was like the rock slamming through her heart.

"Zane," she managed. Zane was the last person she'd ever expected to meet on the streets of Mule Hollow. The last person she'd ever *wanted* to meet anywhere ever again! "*What* are you doing here?" she demanded.

"I, well, I moved in last night."

His eyes, his unforgettable, gold-dust eyes, leveled on her as the words *moved in* hit home. Her eyes widened.

"I'm the new deputy in town."

"Deputy—" She yanked from his touch. Fought to appear calm. Fought to appear casual. Fought not to notice how good the years had been to him—that he was as handsome as she'd remembered and just as rugged. His cheekbones were more prominent, his jaw harder, his lips... Her mouth went dry. "You're *living* here?" she repeated. *Repeated,* as though he hadn't just said it loud and clear.

He nodded, probably thinking she'd lost her mind in the years since they'd had their...since their paths had crossed. Humiliation swamped her and she felt her cheeks heat as her past opened like a yawning black hole and threatened to swallow her. For a brief instant she almost welcomed the refuge fainting would give her. But weakness wasn't an option. Weakness was a weapon that she'd sworn no one would ever use against her again.

"Where?"

He jerked his head to the right. "I moved into the apartment up there."

Her gaze followed his to the apartment above the

real estate office. It was directly across the street from the dress store where she worked!

Rose wasn't a good enough actress to hide her shock. "I see." *No, I don't,* she silently said. *What are you doing here?*

"It's been a long time, Rose. How are you?"

How are you? After all they'd been through and all that had happened between them... What kind of question was that? This man had torn her world apart and now he wanted to make small talk! Her insides rolled. "Fine," she blurted. "Mule Hollow is a great place." How was she chatting when she wanted to throw up? Pass out. Run.

"That's what I hear," he said, his gaze searching hers. "Here, do you want me to take those for you?"

"No!" she exclaimed, and jerked away. Experiencing his touch again was the last thing she wanted. She was amazed she didn't drop her packages. More amazed she didn't throw them at him.

"I—I really need to be going. I have to get to work. But I'm sure we'll see each other again. This is a small town."

Too small for the both of them, she thought, angling past him.

"That's what I'm counting on."

She managed a nod, then hurried across the street to the dress store. She was off today, but she'd forgotten momentarily that her car was parked in front of the feed store. Her only thought was getting away. She wasn't sure how her legs held her up, but she made it across the street and to the door.

"Hang on," she growled under her breath. Her hand shook violently as she grasped the doorknob, wrestled with her packages and at the same time somehow got inside. She kicked the door closed just as her arms turned into noodles and the boxes toppled to the ground. Struggling to breathe, she fell against the wall and fought to regain some sort of control. It was a hard thing to do when everything she cared about was now at risk.

Zane Cantrell was *here.*

Zane watched Rose disappear inside Ashby's Treasures. He wasn't certain if he'd been right in coming here, but one look into her midnight-blue eyes told him he'd done what he needed to do. He wasn't surprised that she hadn't been glad to see him. He was trained to read people, but it hadn't taken a trained eye to see that he'd upset her. An expected reaction, considering the likelihood she hated him.

And with reason.

Chapter Two

What are dreams made of?

Standing in the center of the pasture surrounding her newly acquired home, Rose smiled despite the turmoil she was feeling since seeing *him* that morning. Not many would say their dreams were made of ugly, purple, egg-shaped fruit. But that was exactly what Rose's dreams were made of. Delicious prickly pear fruit.

The house was old and the pastures were overrun with huge prickly pear cacti. To the town it looked about the most useless of any land the Lord had ever created. But that was precisely the reason she'd saved and worked to buy this particular piece of property. These heavily laden plants, whose beautiful yellow flowers had given way to the ugly fruit, were a thing of beauty. They were her field of dreams.

She and Max had arrived in Mule Hollow on a bus loaded with other women relocating from a burned-down women's shelter in L.A. They'd come with the hope that the small town and the new women's shelter might be the answer to their prayers.

It had been everything they'd hoped and so much more. The town had such a caring, loving need to make the newcomers feel safe and that they had something to offer the community. That made a difference. Especially for Max. He'd taken to the town almost immediately and now dreamed of owning his own ranch one day. On the streets of L.A. that thought would have never crossed his mind. She thanked God every day for leading them here.

And this—this deceptive-looking field of cacti surrounding this frame house and barn that had seen better days—this was where their dreams were going to come true.

She refused to think the past few hours could have changed that.

"Mom!" Max yelled.

She spun and watched her gangly teenage son zigzag toward her through the cacti. In his gloved hand he held a canvas bag aloft like the trophy that it was.

"I've got a bagful," he said, skidding to a halt, his beautiful eyes sparkling from behind the protective goggles. She could hear the grin in his voice behind the bandana covering the rest of his face. The tiny, hairlike stingers on the fruit and the cactus plant were not something to take chances with. They were horribly irritating if they got on skin; in the eyes would be even worse. He'd grumbled when she'd first asked him to wear the goggles, but no protective wear, no deal. When she'd gotten home from town he'd been so anxious to get to work he hadn't blinked twice as he'd snapped the goggles into place.

He was too excited about the prospect of harvesting the fruit to notice that she was upset. She was glad because, though she tried to hide it, there had still been the chance that her observant son might notice. She wasn't ready to explain Zane...*Mule Hollow's new deputy!*

Her temperature rose at the thought of him.

Desperately in need of a distraction, she stood dressed in her own gear harvesting prickly pear. Just what she needed. Denial was the name of the game. And at the moment, she'd play the game, because Zane, here in Mule Hollow, was simply too overwhelming to take in one dose.

She needed time to process it. Needed time to find a way to explain it all to Max. He knew that they'd spent many years in one shelter after the other, but he didn't know all the circumstances that had led up to their nomadic way of life. He didn't know that she'd witnessed a murder when she was twenty. Or that she'd briefly entered the witness protection program, when her testimony had sent the killer to prison. Nor did he know the whole truth about why or how she'd taken back her real name.

Max had been too young to remember anything of that life and she wanted to keep it that way.

Forcing the thoughts away, she held up her matching bag of fruit. "Me, too," she said. "But, Max, please slow down. If you trip and fall into a cactus, those bristles are going to eat you alive."

He tugged the bandana down. "Mom, stop worrying. I'm covered up like a mummy. Besides, I *don't* trip." The words were spoken like only a cocky teenager could do. "I'm an entrepreneur. The guys still can't believe I'm opening my own business at *fourteen.*"

Rose teasingly lifted a brow at his words, loving his

willingness to succeed. He was a fighter. Ambitious to achieve his goals. He was as proud as she was to have their first home, because at his young age he knew what it meant not to have a place to call their own. His ambition would help him survive.

"*We're* opening a business," he amended with a wide grin and teasing brow of his own. "Just you and me, kid," he said with a wink of his beautiful golden eyes.

Instantly a stab of worry cut Rose to the core. Those eyes coupled with that wide grin… She was standing on top of a house of cards that had already begun to buckle.

But not here. Not in this moment when everything was supposed to be so perfect. "We're full partners," she said, forcing the conversation forward. "You are welcome to be as involved in this as you want to be. I'm going to rely on you a lot. If you're sure you want the responsibilities."

His eyes turned serious in an instant. "I'm in all the way. Remember, I have a ranch to buy. That means I better get to work. It's torch time." He took her bag, then sauntered off toward the worktable where his torches waited.

Cleaning off the stickers required singeing the bristles off with the hot flame. Like Pete said, it was a guy thing.

Watching him, panic crowded near. Zane was *here*. In her town.

She could run, leave all of this behind—but she couldn't do that to Max. She sucked in a shaky breath, attempting to calm her fears. Deep down she'd feared this day might come. And now that it was here there was only one thing she could do.

Stay put.

No more running.

It was time to make a stand, whether she was ready to or not.

"I still can't believe we got ourselves a real live Texas Ranger as a deputy in our little town," Applegate Thornton said, sounding like he was talking through a bullhorn the minute Zane entered Sam's Diner. Applegate was a reedy, dour elderly man of average height—Zane figured his scarecrow thinness probably made him seem taller to most on first glance. He was a mainstay of Sam's Diner. With his buddy Stanley Orr, he seemed to have the pulse of the community well in hand. They sat front and center at the window table and were deep into their morning checker tournament. Zane had met them the previous day after his encounter with Rose. The two men and Sam had practically interrogated him for an hour.

It was pretty evident to Zane that though they looked like they were engrossed in their game, their eagle eyes saw everything that happened on the street beyond their window.

Softer, shorter and smiling, Stanley nodded in agreement. "Brady's a good man, too. I bet he'd a made a good Ranger. Hard ta b'lieve our little town's been fortunate ta get y'all both."

"I appreciate the vote of confidence," Zane said, with a nod their direction. It was true. He'd only been in the small town a couple of days, but he already felt a connection to it. His natural sense of protectiveness had gone on full alert. Not that he was expecting any trouble—but if it came calling he'd meet it head-on. Zane had never taken his job lightly, as a Ranger or now, as a sworn deputy. He'd always prided himself on making choices in the best interests of the people or places entrusted in his care. For the most part, that code had left him with few regrets and enabled him to be proud of looking back. Rose was the exception.

"So, what do the two of you do?" he asked.

Sam hustled from the kitchen with tray of clean coffee cups. He was five feet, if that, with the bow-legged gait of a man who'd been built to sit a horse. Zane saw the craggy-faced proprietor as a small man with a big heart and more than likely a tenacious one. There was something about his eyes and his stout hand-shake that spoke to Zane. He was a mainstay of the community. Zane had studied people all his life, and then trained for it in his job, but there were some people who wore their character like an open book for all the world to see—that was Sam Green. He was a man who could be counted on. It was the way Zane had always hoped he could be described by those who knew him. It cut deep that Rose couldn't say that about him.

"Them two," Sam said, indicating Applegate and Stanley with a nod and talking loud enough for them to hear his every word. "Don't let 'm fool ya. They kin get into more trouble than two teenagers let loose fer the first time in thar daddy's pickup."

Zane chuckled. "That so?"

Applegate scowled from across the room. "No mor'n anybody else. We're retired and plum tired of it. So now we help out at The Barn Theater on the out-skirts of town and that fills some of'r time."

"That's right." Stanley jumped one of his checkers over Applegate's, winning him a hard look. "You'll have ta come on out and take in a show. We got our-selves a right smart good program."

Applegate grinned for the first time and surprised Zane so much by the transformation that he almost spit out the coffee he'd just taken a sip of.

"Got some mighty fine talent out thar. Why we got *re*viewed in pert near ever newspaper that's worth its salt. And our Sugar Rae Denton even got invited to be in a movie and on Broadway!"

"I'm impressed," Zane said.

Sam arched a brow. "We got all kinds of good thangs going on in this little town. One of them thangs is my wife and her two friends. You bein' a single man, ya ought to be prepared ta draw their special attentions."

"Why do I get the feeling you've had this conversation several times in the past?" He knew resident journalist, Molly Jacobs, wrote a syndicated newspaper column about the goings-on of the town. He had heard it frequently covered matchmaking.

"'Cuz it's true," Applegate grunted, then plopped a handful of sunflower seeds into his mouth and grinned. He was more amiable than Zane had first taken him to be. "And it kin be downright entertainin' fer us old-timers ta see you young bucks get snared up in their good intentions. Ain't that so, Stanley?"

"Yup. This here spot in front of this window is better seat'n than front row at one of them movie theaters."

Sam grinned at Zane. "We figure'd ta warn ya and then sit back and watch the show when they start in on ya."

Their candor caused Zane to laugh, but it faded quickly when the older men all stared at him funny.

"Did I do something wrong?" he asked, feeling suddenly like he was in a lineup.

Stanley pulled at his ear. "When you laugh like that, I seemed ta thank maybe I met you someplace b'fore."

"Yeah," Applegate agreed.

Sam nodded. "But I ain't one ta forget faces, so I know I ain't met you."

Zane had had his fair share of so-called twins through the years. He was certain everyone got told several times in their life that they looked just like someone else. "Someone in this area must resemble me," he offered.

"That must be it," Sam said, rubbing his chin and continuing to study Zane.

"We know e'vrbody," Applegate grunted, piercing Zane with his scrutiny. "Who do y'all thank it is?"

"Cain't put a finger on it," Stanley mumbled. "But it's that smile and something else… I jest cain't figure it out."

Zane chuckled. "Well, boys, relax. Given the size of Mule Hollow, one of us is bound to run into my look-alike pretty quick. When we do, the mystery will be solved."

Zane, who was used to challenging jobs, figured that would be the biggest mystery he might face in the peaceful little community. It was going to take some getting used to. But if he could make things right with Rose, then he would gladly settle into this quiet life with a happy heart.

Chapter Three

Mule Hollow was having a baby and everyone was in an uproar! For a town that had been on the verge of dying not so very long ago, it was pure joy to think that babies were coming. Rose couldn't miss Dottie's shower, no matter how much she'd considered hiding out at home. Dottie had been on bed rest for a month, so the shower was being held at her home. The place was packed with women.

Even though Rose was apprehensive about what was going to happen with Zane, she was determined to go on as if her world hadn't been turned upside down.

As she'd done with Max in the cactus field, she focused on what was going on around her. It was always lively when the women of Mule Hollow got together. So unlike her own silent, secretive pregnancy. The comparison slipped in unbidden; it was as if Zane coming into her life again had brought her past back to haunt her. By the time she was as far along as Dottie, Rose realized she'd gotten herself into a mess. By this time she'd stopped thinking David, her ex-husband, was the answer to her troubles. By then he'd begun to show his true colors and she was regretting her rash decision to marry him. His overprotectiveness had first drawn her to him, but she'd soon learned it was control and not care that drove him. Almost the instant their vows were spoken, he'd begun shutting her in and shutting out the world. She made no friends and even if she had, he wouldn't have allowed them to come around. A gathering like this wouldn't have happened.

"This is from Norma Sue," Dottie said, reading the card. She was sitting on the couch and melted as she pulled back the tissue paper, exposing a pair of red, satin baby slippers and a matching dress. "Ohhh," she cooed, lifting them for everyone to see.

"I love red!" Scarlet-haired Esther Mae's voice rose above the others' exclamations. Esther Mae was in her sixties and as vibrant as the color she dyed her hair. "Every baby girl needs a red outfit. You did good, Norma."

Her friend and cohort in all kinds of escapades, Norma Sue Jenkins's plump cheeks beamed. "I figured if the baby has a head of black hair like Dottie, that the red would look real nice."

"You are so right," Dottie sighed, her navy eyes bright against her pale skin. She handed the gift off and it began to make its trip around the room.

"This is from Lacy," Rose said, glancing at the card on the bag, then holding it toward Dottie. Her hand was resting on her rounded stomach and she looked slightly uncomfortable. Rose hesitated. "Are you okay? Not too tired?"

"I'm fine. Really," she said, but didn't look completely convincing.

Rose hadn't been ill a single day while she was carrying Max, a blessing in more ways than one. Her life had been so messed up in other ways that she'd been thankful not to add morning sickness to the mix. Still, she felt for Dottie.

"You do look tired," Lacy Matlock said. Live-wire Lacy had enough energy to share with anyone who needed it. "Is there anything we can do to help you more?"

All the ladies seemed to lean forward, reminding Rose of racers in the starting blocks. Rose got the sudden picture of Dottie saying she could use a glass of water and the entire room blasting forward to get it for her. It was a sweet picture and so like her town. A lump formed in her throat. Her emotions were unusually volatile today. What would it have been like to have had this kind of support when Max had been born?

"Please don't worry about me," Dottie urged everyone. "The doctor assures me that the lack of energy is nothing to get worried about. You all know, my body went through an ordeal in that hurricane in Florida. He said considering all that my poor body had been through that I'm doing great. God has me in the palm of His hand."

"Yes, you are, my dear," Adela said. She was a wisp of a woman with a snowy-white pixie cut, and together with Norma Sue and Esther Mae completed the notorious matchmaking posse of Mule Hollow.

Esther Mae relaxed. "Y'all are right. My goodness, Dottie, the good Lord brought you through being crushed under that house so I expect He's got bringing our sweet baby into the world under control."

Rose let those words sink in. God was in control of

her life, too…but she couldn't help feeling like she was riding in a car without brakes. She managed to make it through the present opening without letting her thoughts dwell on Zane. However, a few minutes later, while everyone was enjoying cookies and punch, that became impossible when talk turned suddenly to the new deputy in town. Of course it would—she should have expected it. Not much went on in a small town that didn't get talked about and a new deputy, especially a handsome ex-Texas Ranger, would draw attention. Rose had half expected it to be one of the matchmakers who brought him up, but it was Dottie.

"I'm so happy to have Zane helping Brady out," Dottie said as she sipped her strawberry punch.

"He seems like a real nice, upstanding man," Norma Sue said. "And he's single."

"And *sooo* good-looking," Esther Mae added. "I met him yesterday. He has the most intense eyes. I mean really, they just come alive with all that gold sparking them up. It just gave me goose bumps when he looked at me."

"They are unique," Norma Sue added. "Just think how they'll light up when the right woman comes along!"

If Rose hadn't been so upset she might have gotten tickled watching the matchmakers setting their sights on a fresh target. But that wasn't the case. As she took a long drink of her punch, she was too busy trying to keep her hand from shaking while the fear she'd been trying to deny began to surface. Zane's eyes were unique—but she saw a similar set across the dinner table every night. Would they realize?

All the questions that she was trying to put off suddenly came screaming forward. His coming here couldn't be an accident. He had to have discovered she lived here. But why had he followed her here after all these years?

Did he know?

The question knocked the breath out of Rose. Panic hit her and she hurried to the kitchen. Her hand was shaking and as she set her cup down punch sloshed onto the counter.

"You okay?"

She jumped, startled as Lacy came through the doorway behind her.

"You look as white as the tablecloth."

Panic clawed at Rose. "I—I need to go. Could you tell the others I had to leave?" She was already headed toward the door. She could feel her friend watching her. She knew Lacy would be worried about her, but Rose was too distraught to attempt a smoother exit. The denial she'd been struggling to keep at bay came down on her head in a landslide.

What had she been thinking? She couldn't put her head in the sand and pretend this wasn't happening. She had to confront Zane and she had to do it now.

She had to find out what had brought him to Mule Hollow.

She had to find out if he knew her secret.

"Thank you, Officer Cantrell. You saved my life."

"You're welcome, Mrs. Lovelace. But all I did was change your tire." Zane stepped back from the SUV and tipped his hat to the petite brunette. From the backseat the excited barks of two miniature poodles erupted.

"Oh, you saved me all right. If you hadn't come along when you did, me and my babies wouldn't have been able to make it to San Antonio in time for registration."

"Drive safe. You've got plenty of time." Zane waved as Mrs. Lovelace and her barking menagerie headed off in pursuit of dog-show glory. He was grinning as he got into his truck and drove back toward town. So far during his first couple of days at work, he hadn't done much of anything. This roadside rescue was his first actual official act. Brady had assured him that the job had its days when everything happened at once. He was supposed to expect the unexpected at any given moment.

Mrs. Lovelace had been distraught when he'd found her broken down on the side of the road. With no phone service for her to call for help and absolutely no idea how to change a flat, she had been more than happy to see him drive up. Three months ago, he'd been escorting a federal criminal into court, and today he was sending poodles to dog shows.

It was a little hard to get used to, and as he drove into town, Zane wondered if he was going to be able to make this adjustment.

He was surprised but pleased to find Rose standing outside the sheriff's office when he drove up. Just as it had the first time he'd seen her all those years ago, every protective instinct he had went into high gear when it came to this woman. The first time he'd met her she'd been a scared young woman who'd witnessed a murder. There had been no hysterics or melodrama. She'd quietly come forward and told her story, though she'd been visibly shaken. He'd greatly admired her for stepping up when it would have been easier…*safer* to pretend she hadn't seen anything.

"Why are you here?" she demanded.

The anger in her voice jolted him. Even though it was well-deserved and expected. He stepped to the pavement, closing his door behind him as he grappled with the right words. She kept on talking.

"You can't tell me that you showing up here was an accident. Mule Hollow is just too small. Too out of the way. And after all these years, why?"

There was a fierceness in her eyes that he'd not seen before. He'd known he wouldn't be welcome. "I had to come try to make things right between us."

She gave him a look of disgust. He'd told himself he was prepared for this reaction, but he wasn't. Beautiful, sweet Rose looking this hostile broke his heart. How could he have expected her to understand what he'd done? Why he'd done it? He'd never given her any explanation of why he'd left. Up until this moment he hadn't realized that deep down he'd hoped his leaving hadn't affected her. Knowing he'd embittered her like this was hard to take.

"Make things right?" she scoffed at last. "Why now, Zane? That was the past and you of all people should know that I don't live in the past. After all, *you* were the one who taught me the art of living a lie."

"That was my job. It was to keep you safe and you know it. Taking on a new identity was the only way. You had to, or you might have been killed before you testified against that thug, Lawton." He knew this wasn't really what she was asking yet he needed to get his head back on straight. It was not keeping her safe that he needed forgiveness for. His oath required him to protect those under his care, but with Rose it had gone so much deeper. From day one of meeting her he'd been doomed.

When he'd been assigned to Rose's case, it had

been his job to explain her options. He'd explained that she needed to enter the program or risk being killed before she could testify. Rose had touched his heart with the way she'd handled herself. Naively, without understanding what it would cost her, she agreed to do what was needed to see justice served. She hadn't realized her ailing grandmother would refuse to go into the program with her. It had been a devastating blow to Rose. He'd had to stand at the door and watch as her grandmother sent her away. She'd believed, and rightly so, that her illness might somehow make it easier for Rose to be tracked down. It had killed Rose to say goodbye, but it was her grandmother's wish that Rose be safe. And against his better judgment, for the first time in his life his job became personal.

It went beyond his oath, beyond the promise to her grandmother that he would keep her safe at all cost…he'd fallen in love with Rose, with her principles, with her loyalty. And she'd almost lost her life because of it.

"I did what had to be done to keep you safe," he said. And it was true, even down to leaving her. It was putting her at risk and not telling her goodbye that he needed to make right.

Rose stared at Zane. Hearing him say he'd done what he'd thought was best to keep her safe cut to the quick. After all these years, how could it still hurt so much?

"We need to get some things straight," she said, hearing the bitterness in her voice. "Have you told anyone that we know each other?" If no one knew, then maybe she had a little more time to figure things out. But she had to know if he knew about Max and had come looking for him.

"No," he said, unlocking the door. "Let's go inside."

Rose didn't want to be alone in a room with him. But what she needed to say shouldn't be discussed on the street, so she nodded.

She refused to let him see her unravel. But looking into his amber eyes so dusted with flecks of gold that they stood out in a crowd made it near impossible. She felt certain everyone in Mule Hollow was going to see that Zane Cantrell had given his son his distinctive eyes.

And if that weren't enough, he'd passed his devastating smile to Max as well.

Rose felt sick and her legs barely held her up long enough to walk past Zane to the chair in front of his desk. "I've started a new life here, Zane," she managed while she sank into the chair. "This one is real. I don't want to be reminded of my past. Of the lies. My son doesn't know I was once in the witness protection program and I had hoped to keep it that way. I wanted him to be…one identity. His real identity." Only he doesn't know his real identity.

Rose inhaled sharply. Her blood pounded in her temples. Until Zane had come into the picture she'd been able to pretend that Max didn't need to know the truth.

Zane sat on the edge of the desk and looked down at her. Despite everything between them, her insides knotted with the pull of emotions. Oh, how she'd loved this man before he'd abandoned her.

Abruptly, he moved from the desk to the window and stood gazing out, with his back to her.

Did he know?

She wasn't sure how well the U.S. Marshal's office kept up with witnesses after they were deemed safe to return to the world as they'd known it. And she wasn't certain how much information a Ranger assigned to the case would have access to. How much of her life since the last time they'd seen each other did Zane know?

His wide shoulders remained rigid as moments ticked by and he stared out the window. When he turned back to her, his expression gave nothing away. Striding past her, he took his seat behind the desk. "I'm not sure I understand why you'd keep your past hidden," he said finally. "What you did was a brave thing. It's something to be proud of. Since there is no threat any longer, no one would be in danger from knowing the truth."

He didn't know! Relief washed over Rose at the realization. She suddenly felt light-headed and closed her eyes.

"Are you all right?"

Startled by the concern in his voice, she opened her eyes and nodded. "Yes," she said, trying to get a hold on her emotions. He didn't know Max was his son. If he did he would understand that she wasn't hiding her life in the witness protection program all these years. She'd been hiding from him.

He studied her, his keen eyes searching for the truth in her expression. "Look, Rose. I came here hoping to start over, too. Hoping that we—"

At his admission her traitorous heart beat a little faster. It upset her all the more. "'We,'" she gasped. "There is no 'we.' Will never be a 'we.'"

"We" died the day you left me there…alone.

The muscle in his jaw jerked and his gaze darkened.

"I see," he said after a long moment. "Coming here and seeing that you're okay has been worth it. I would never do anything to jeopardize your happiness."

There was so much she wanted to say to him. But she wouldn't. She'd believed she was over being bitter…but she was seeing the truth now. "I hope not. But if you'll remember, I don't have much faith in what you say."

His expression hardened. "I did what I considered was right for you when I got reassigned. I believed it would keep you safe. I'd do it all over again if I felt it was the best choice."

She surged to her feet, emotions rushing at her like darts. "I *trusted* you, Zane. Do you even know what that means?" She was mortified at knowing she was about to unravel in front of him. "I can't do this. I just needed to get things out in the open between us. Stay away from me and my son. Like I said, Max has no idea about my life in the witness protection program. I chose not to tell him because we've had more than our share of bad luck and I feel as if I've spent my entire life in hiding. I didn't want him to feel that way. Your coming here can only make things bad again." She closed her eyes and fought down the fear of what would come if he stayed. It was an impossible situation. "Stay away," she managed as she headed toward the door.

Zane was beside her in an instant, his hand reaching to open the door for her, surprising her with his apologetic smile…Max's smile.

"I can't do that, Rose. I owe it to you to explain. To make you see—"

"I don't want anything from you. It's too late for explanations." There, that was plain enough. Back stiff, she walked out the door. But she knew when she got inside her car and met Zane's unwavering gaze through the windshield that somehow what she wanted didn't matter. Never had. Zane would do what he wanted and she would suffer the consequences.

Chapter Four

"You feeling okay, Mom?" Max asked as they got out of the car and started toward the church the next morning.

"I'm fine. Just a little tired, I think," Rose said, feeling as if she was walking straight into disaster. She should have told Max last night. "I was up late making syrup for the jelly." And worrying—but she kept that thought to herself as she looked up at her son. Even at his age it was obvious he was going to be tall and lean just like…his dad. All these years she'd tried to pretend she didn't see Zane every time she looked at Max, but that was impossible. And today, with each step she took toward the small crowd gathered on the church lawn, her world teetered on the edge of falling apart.

What would Max say when he realized that she'd lied to him? The very idea made her sick. Her skin was clammy and her stomach kept lurching as if she were on a raft in high seas. Seeing Zane standing among her friends sent her hand to her stomach in the futile attempt to quell the queasiness. She'd left his office the day before knowing she'd left herself wide open for a public confrontation. She'd like to think that even if Zane realized the truth, he wouldn't make a scene…but she didn't really know him. It was stupid on her part, but she really wasn't thinking straight. How did a woman break such news to her son? She prayed God would help her figure this out. So far no light had appeared at the end of the long, dark tunnel she found herself in.

"Hey, there's Gil. I'll check ya later." Max loped away.

She watched him go and felt a touch of relief knowing the inevitable might have been put off for a few minutes. Why hadn't she figured out a way to tell him?

"Rose, over here," Norma Sue hollered, waving her over. Rose paused and engrossed herself in digging a peppermint out of her purse. It was her only excuse for delaying moving toward Zane. Also, peppermint was good for a queasy stomach. Her fingers trembled as she unwrapped the candy and plopped it into her mouth. Sadly, there was no instant calm for her nerves.

Esther Mae and Norma Sue were both waving her forward now, with big rolling waves like traffic cops. She nodded and finally, with nothing else to put it off, she closed her eyes, prayed for guidance—intervention actually—and then willed herself to cross the yard.

You can do this, she coached herself.

She *would* do this. *Could* do this.

Deep breath. Another deep breath and steps in between had her moving across the lawn. Choices from the past yielded consequences—the truth exposed was of her own making. She'd lived almost half her life behind a mask of deception and as much as she despised it, she would do it for a bit longer if it meant clinging to her and Max's make-believe life for a moment more.

She couldn't help clinging to it for as long as possible, because she was terrified of how their relationship would forever be altered when he realized she'd lied to him.

Zane had been watching her approach, but she'd kept her gaze off him. Meeting his watchful stare would only make her queasiness worse—throwing up on the church lawn was not something she wanted to do. Thank goodness for the peppermint, though she realized she was really expecting a lot from the tiny piece of candy.

"Good morning," she said, pleased that her voice sounded halfway normal. She continued to avoid Zane's piercing gaze locked onto her like a missile to a target. Of course he had no idea the potentially explosive nature of their meeting here on the lawn of the quaint country church.

Rose scanned the small crowd. Who would discover her secret first? Who would recognize what they were looking at? The question loomed over her like a monster's shadow—who would unwittingly expose her?

"How are you feeling today?" Esther Mae asked. She had on a pillbox hat with white and orange daisies and Rose concentrated on the flowers. It was a very subdued hat compared to Esther Mae's favorite with big purple feathers. Sadly for Rose, the daisies weren't distracting enough for her needs.

"Feeling?" she asked, trying to focus on why they were asking her how she was feeling.

"Yes, you left the shower so fast yesterday we worried you might have caught a bug or something."

"Oh, that." She was breathless and gave Esther Mae

what she feared was a pitiful attempt of a smile. "Fine. I'm fine. Really," she rambled, while her betraying gaze slid to Zane. He might seem at ease to the group, but she saw the keen watchful alertness in his lawman's eyes and knew he was looking much deeper. Knew he understood she was on pins and needles. He just didn't know why. She looked from Esther Mae to Norma Sue. "No bug here." She forced a laugh that came off sounding exactly like the nervous laugh it was. "Just another case of prickly pear jam that needed to be put up," she said lightly, when in reality her knees were buckling and she needed to lie down. No, what she needed was a little backbone.

"Zane, you are definitely going to have to try some of Rose's jam," Norma Sue said. "It's good enough to make a grown man cry—"

"That's the truth," Esther Mae gushed. "Our Rose is the catch of the county. A cowboy would snatch her up in a second if he had any brains beneath his Stetson!"

"Is that right?" Zane asked, a chuckle underscoring his words. His grave eyes twinkled.

The heat of mortification flared across Rose's clammy skin. Things couldn't get any worse. But of course she knew they could…*would*.

Norma Sue didn't even try to hide her matchmaking attempt. "Matter of fact, Rose has just gotten moved into her very own place out there in the country. It would probably be a good idea for you to keep a close watch on her place when you're out making your rounds. You know, her being a single woman and all."

"No!" Rose exclaimed. "Norma, I'm quite capable

of taking care of myself," she stammered over the candy in her mouth.

Zane had on his poker face, but she could tell he was amused as he crossed his arms and studied her. The way he used to. All those years ago, when they first met and she was an idealistic, naive twenty-year-old, and he was her sworn protector. What a lie that had been. It made her temperature boil and her spine stiffen. "Deputy Cantrell won't have any reason for stopping by my place, I can assure you." She gave him a cool look that caused Esther Mae to gasp and Norma Sue's brows to dip in consternation. Since coming to Mule Hollow she'd been nothing but grateful and thrilled to be here. She didn't like this side of herself and didn't appreciate Zane for coming here and provoking her!

"When you need help, you just call," Zane said, as if he hadn't heard her jibe! "I'll be there for you. I promise."

Oh, right, just like before. Rose went straight from feeling sick to furious. "I'm sure all of Mule Hollow will rest easier knowing you are *so* very reliable," she practically sneered. Her sarcasm was so unlike her that it brought another gasp from Esther Mae.

"W-we certainly will," Norma Sue said, finally getting over her uncharacteristic loss of words. Looking from Rose to Zane, she grinned so wide her plump cheeks almost touched her eyes. "We were just telling Zane that he reminds us of someone. What do you think?" She slapped her hands on her ample hips and studied him intently. "You got any ideas, Rose?"

Rose's heart plummeted as her fear replaced everything. This was it. She could see Max written all over Zane, not only his smile and his eyes, but in the way

he stood, the tone of his voice… There was no way—
no way—she was the only one who could see this!
What could she say?

The corner of Zane's lips lifted. "Applegate,
Stanley and Sam thought the same thing. I guess I have
a twin."

Rose clamped her teeth together, sending the peppermint right down her windpipe!

She wheezed and her eyes watered.

Norma Sue slapped her on the back. "You okay?"

"Y-yes," she gasped as her mind whirled. She had
to act. Had to do something before they figured it out
right then and there. She needed a little more time.
"Oh, goodness, it's time for class," she gushed and
grabbed Zane's arm. "Come with me. I'll show you
to our classroom. I'm sure Sheriff Brady already informed you that he's the teacher of the singles class,"
she said, tugging him along. "Bye, ladies," she called
over her shoulder, then frowned up at Zane. He was
looking at her like she'd lost her marbles.

The ladies' excited voices carried on the breeze
behind them. "Oh, Norma, that's perfect!" Esther Mae
exclaimed. "Don't they look cute together?"

"Sure do."

The confusion and curiosity in sharp-as-a-tack
Norma Sue's voice caused Rose to cringe, but she
continued to pull Zane along the sidewalk. She
ignored the surprise she'd seen in his eyes. She knew
full well that her escorting him around was the last
thing he'd expected. He was a lawman through and
through and had to be wondering why she was acting
so erratically.

She had to pull herself together. But she also
couldn't just stand there and wait while Norma and
Esther put two and two together. This was all she

could come up with. "Don't look at me that way," she snapped, dragging him on with little resistance.

"And how would that be?"

"Like I've lost my mind."

He chuckled, a low rumble that sent her senses tumbling. "Have you?"

She turned on him a few feet from the annex entrance. "No. I certainly have not," she hissed, leaning close so no one would hear. "You know very well it is your impromptu visit that has me choking on peppermints. Sweating bullets. Acting like an ill-mannered—"

"*Rose.* Calm down."

"Don't tell me to calm down. You've come barging into my life. My territory. With no consideration for the life I'm building here."

"Rose, I'm sorry."

He took her by the shoulders and she froze at his touch; his palms were warm against her bare skin and sent shivers racing through her.

"I tried to explain. You wouldn't let me. Would you look at me? Please."

Reluctantly, Rose did as he asked. It was a bad move, because looking at Zane almost made her believe he was sincere. And if there was one thing she'd learned about Zane Cantrell, it was to never believe he was sincere.

Even after all this time the realization had the ability to knock the breath out of her. It bothered her that he could still have that power. "We need to go inside," she said. Pulling away from his touch, she yanked open the door and led the way into the building.

Her life was falling apart and she didn't know what to do!

* * *

Brady had been the first to invite Zane to church when he'd arrived in town. Zane tried to concentrate on the lesson Brady was teaching, but it was useless because all he could think about was that Rose hated him.

He wasn't sure why she'd dragged him into the class with her in the first place. Not when it was clear that him jumping off the edge of the world would have been her first choice.

The woman's scorn was epic.

That they'd very nearly had an altercation out in front of the church hadn't been something he'd been prepared for. The Rose he'd known and loved had been idealistic, warmhearted—spirited, yes, but unbelievably gentle. He didn't know the Rose sitting rigidly beside him.

Earlier, he'd watched her and her son as they'd exited their car and then walked across the gravel parking lot toward the church. She hadn't looked happy even then. Though he hadn't gotten a close look at her son before he'd disappeared inside the annex, he'd been surprised to realize how tall the youth was.

He had to admit that it was hard to realize that Rose had a teenage son. Seeing her with a child was another reminder of all the years Zane had foolishly let stretch between them. He had a bad feeling that his coming to Mule Hollow was a futile attempt and that no reconciliation would be had between him and the only woman he'd ever loved.

He'd known he had his work cut out for him when he came searching for her. And he'd been right.

Chapter Five

The instant Brady finished giving the final prayer, Rose left the classroom. The hallway was packed as everyone headed toward the exits before walking up the sidewalk to the front of the church for morning services.

Rose greeted everyone she had to, but was intent on getting outside and going home. No church for her today. She'd realized she couldn't continue this way. She had to get Max home and come clean.

Her throat clogged thinking about what he was going to do. She'd lied to him about one of the most important things in his life. Rose knew now that she couldn't take the chance on it coming out before she'd told him. Maybe she was just being paranoid thinking anyone other than Zane could possibly put the pieces together. Who could do that? No one even knew they'd known each other before. Still, irrational as it was, the fear clung to her.

Dear Lord, help me, she prayed as she walked outside. *Help me.* She felt like such a hypocrite asking for help when she'd been so wrong in everything she'd done.

She could hear Zane behind her at the door as he was greeted by people. The man had only been in town a few days and already seemed to know everyone. She scanned the lawn, looking for Max. She had to get to him. Not seeing him, she turned to search behind her in the moving crowd. No Max. Instead she found herself looking straight at Zane. He was mere inches from her and his eyes were troubled.

"We really need to talk," he said quietly, leaning close. "This is not the way things need to be."

She swallowed hard. He had no idea the strain that was weighing on her. Before she could say anything more, Esther Mae and Norma Sue were back upon them.

"Zane, yoo-hoo!" Esther Mae said, waving as she plowed the way in front of Norma Sue. "We just had to come look at you again. We can almost see who it is you look like, but it won't come to us." Barreling to a halt, they studied him as though he was the latest exhibit at an art show.

Rose wanted to yell fire or something! Anything to prevent this scrutiny. Her gaze slunk from them to Zane. His golden eyes were sparkling as he smiled that devastating smile of his at the older ladies. Rose's adrenaline was pumping so she could hardly breathe. Then from the corner of her eye she saw Applegate and Stanley burst from the annex exit. They headed straight toward them. Rose groaned because their keen eyes were glued to Zane as they stopped before him. And her nightmare was about to come full circle, because Max and his friend Gil were coming out of the annex, too.

"I told ya, Stanley. I told ya," Applegate said. "Don't ya see it? Jest look close. It's jest plain uncanny. That's what it is."

Stanley scratched his bald spot and his eyes wid-

ened. "Well, what do ya know? Yor plum right, App."
Both men looked from Zane to Max, who was ap-
proaching Rose and the rest of the gathering crowd.
Rose was heading for the edge of Niagara Falls. There
was nothing humanly possible that she could do to
stop going over the edge.

Max and Gil came to a halt in front of Zane. Oblivi-
ous to everyone's stares, both boys looked at Zane in
awe. Max's eyes glittered gold in the sunlight. He
might as well have been wearing a sign proclaiming his
identity.

"You must be the new deputy. The Texas *Ranger.*
This is Gil and I'm Max." He smiled openly at Zane.

The admiration in his warm eyes caused a deep
ache in Rose's heart. Her son had just met his dad and
he had no idea… Shame engulfed her. Max believed
his dad was a lowlife they'd had to escape and then
hide from for years until he had finally given up hunt-
ing them. He was a man to be ashamed of and feared.
And, now, Max was about to learn that his mother was
a liar. *Dear Lord, what have I done?*

Esther Mae's gasp was loud enough to draw looks
from the far corners of the world. Beside her, Norma
Sue's mouth fell open. Rose felt faint and quickly
scanned the gathering group. Applegate and Stanley
were gaping, too. Of course, none of them realized
exactly what they were seeing—they just saw the startling resemblance.

But she knew that Zane, frozen, his jaw slack, his
brows dipping together over stunned eyes, knew exactly what he was looking at. His son.

Rose had no doubt that he understood what he was
seeing when he tore his gaze from Max and planted
them on her.

"Mom, hey," Max said, breaking into her thoughts. "Do you feel bad? You don't look so good."

Rose grabbed his arm. "I—I need to go home," she stuttered, tugging him back a step, meeting his worried eyes.

"Sure. Maybe you got a bug or something. See y'all later," he said, glancing at the small group.

Rose did the same and didn't miss the stunned looks everyone was still wearing.

"Do you need any help?" Esther Mae asked as did several others. "Maybe Zane could drive you home. You look like you're going to faint."

"No!" The last thing she needed was Zane's help. And one look at the dark expression on his face told her a storm like nothing she'd ever seen was brewing. "I'll be fine." She clung to Max's arm as they headed toward the parking lot. She could feel Zane's eyes boring into her back and was thankful that he chose not to make a scene.

"Everyone sure was looking weird," Max said as soon as they got in the car. "You'd think they never saw a sick woman before. You sure you can drive?"

Rose nodded and proved it by sticking the key in the ignition and twisting. Her hands shook as she put the car in Reverse, but as soon as they were heading out of the parking lot she felt a bit better. Just getting away from Zane for a moment was a relief.

"Did you see the look on Ranger Cantrell's face?" Max asked. "He looked kind of scary. For a minute there I thought I'd done something wrong."

Rose ran over a pothole in the pavement and the car jerked. "Sorry," she gasped as she and Max bounced roughly. "You didn't do anything wrong."

Max laughed. "I figured that out soon as I looked

at you. Who'd have thought a Ranger would be scared of a woman upchucking!"

Rose didn't laugh as she glanced at Max. He was so happy.

He met her eyes. "Mom, what's wrong? You look like you're about to cry," he said, and the smile immediately faded from his face. "Mom?"

Rose inhaled and glued her eyes to the road. How was she going to tell him what was really wrong with Zane?

"Mom, please tell me you aren't fixin' to tell me we're leaving."

"You okay?" Applegate asked. His loud voice added to the pounding in Zane's head. It brought him back to his surroundings and he became aware of Norma Sue and Esther Mae whispering to each other while Applegate and Stanley openly stared at him. They'd seen exactly what he'd seen. But, obviously, they didn't know the truth of it.

They didn't understand that it wasn't some uncanny fluke that Max and him looked so much alike. In reality if it hadn't been for the eyes and the smile they would have only resembled each other like people do. But it was the Cantrell eyes and smile that had them speechless. They didn't know that the genetic pool had been passing that same magnetic smile and glittering, amber eye color to Cantrell men for generations.

He had a *son.*

Rose hadn't said so—she didn't need to. Max was his. It had been like looking at a teenage version of himself. How could this be?

His head was pounding like it would explode. For nearly fifteen years he'd believed that Rose was the most honest woman he'd ever met and her integrity was above reproach. How could she have kept this from him? He focused on the group around him. Focused on covering up the emotions that were raw and exposed.

"I'm fine," he said.

Stanley scratched his head. "That thar is jest plain somethin'. It'd been a shock to me, too, ta see somebody wearin' my face."

"'At's the truth," Applegate grunted. "I told ya him and Max looked alike. It's the eyes and that thar smile."

"The two of you could be related," Esther Mae said. "Me and Norma Sue were speechless there for a minute."

"And that's saying a whole heap." Applegate cocked a bushy gray brow at him. "It jest don't never happen."

Stanley wagged his head to and fro. "Esther Mae's right, though."

"Son, did you and Rose—" Norma Sue began, then slammed her mouth shut and colored slightly. "Forget I said that."

Zane was already walking off, heading for his truck. He had a *son*.

A half-grown son. And it was obvious that Max was as clueless as he was.

"The witness protection program," Max said, clearly confused.

They were sitting in lawn chairs next to the house. It had been as far as Rose's legs could carry her. In the car she'd assured him that they weren't leaving but that she had something very important to tell him, but that it had to wait until they got home. She'd finally forced herself to just say it. Now, she nodded, giving him a moment to process the information.

"But that's for mobsters, isn't it?"

"Not always. Sometimes, innocent bystanders see something that puts them in danger and then they have to go into the program for the protection of themselves and their family. That's what happened to me."

"Wow," he said, interest replacing the confusion in his words. "You saw a murder? Were you scared?"

She nodded again and swallowed the lump forming in her throat.

"And then they saw you and tried to kill you? Like in the movies? Did you have to run? Did they shoot at you?"

His questions flew at her like buckshot. She had to hold her hand up to get him to pause. "It wasn't like that," she said. "The man didn't actually see me. I went to the police and picked him out of a police lineup."

"Cool," Max said. "But how did he know it was you if he didn't see you?"

"He was a very bad man. He had connections. The police had already explained to me that I might have to go into the witness protection program."

"Wow," he said again. "It's just like an episode of *Walker, Texas Ranger!*"

Though Max had loved that popular TV show, she'd never been able to sit through a full episode because it always caused bad memories of Zane to surface. "Sort of," she said, and then answered some of his questions.

"But why didn't Grandma come with you?"

Rose's mother had gotten pregnant just out of high

school and died giving birth to Rose. She'd never known who her dad was. The only people she had in her life were her grandmother and grandfather, who had passed away when she was ten. Though Max hadn't been born before her grandmother died, Rose had told him many stories. She just hadn't told him all of them.

"She couldn't bring herself to leave the house she'd lived in for almost fifty years. It was the home she'd shared with your grandfather. And all of her friends were there."

"But didn't she love you? Didn't she want to be with you?"

"That's the hard part. Yes, she did. But she had health issues, too. And she feared that somehow medical records could lead the man I was hiding from to me."

"Oh. But don't they protect you from all of that?"

"Yes, they do, but things happen. When there is a chance that you've been located they hide you somewhere else. Gram couldn't have handled all the moving. But she wanted me to be safe. Leaving her behind almost killed me. Even now, thinking about it is hard. But the Texas Ranger who helped me explained all of this to us and that was the decision we had to make. We shared letters. They were passed through the Justice Department and when Gram got really ill I was able to see her before she died."

He looked stunned by the information overload. Poor kid had no idea that it only got worse.

"So, are we still in it?" he asked. "I mean, is somebody out there still trying to kill you?"

She shook her head. "Oh, no. We're safe now. All that was before you were born. The man I sent to prison was killed there and so I was able to take back my real name. When I married David I'd been out of the program for about four months."

He studied her and she could see the wheels turning behind his eyes. "So, us always moving—we were really hiding from my dad? All that is real?"

She nodded. She'd had to be honest with him when he was young about the fact that they were hiding from David. He'd had to know not to trust him and not to go anywhere with David if he showed up trying to snatch him. "Unfortunately, that was true, too. Everything about your past is authentic." Rose's panic stole her breath. "Except…"

He straightened, locking his shoulders back and looking so much like his dad. Over the years every time he'd made this move she'd pictured Zane. One day that chest would be wide and strong and those shoulders would look as if they could take on the world.

"You can tell me, Mom. I can handle it," he said, sensing her fear.

She closed her eyes and prayed God would be with the words. Prayed that He would help Max as he took in what she was about to reveal. A tear slipped out and she brushed it away with trembling fingertips.

"Mom—"

She patted his hand and waved off his concern. "Listen, Max. Deputy Cantrell was the Texas Ranger who protected me when I first went into the program—"

"You knew him! Cool. Did you know he was moving here?" Then his expression clouded with confusion. "But wait, you guys didn't say you knew each other."

"No. He didn't tell anyone and I, well, I didn't know

he was coming here until the day I met him on the street. I haven't spoken to him in over fourteen years. Not since he left my case. But—" she stopped and took a deep breath "—I was confused, and scared when I knew Zane. And I made a choice that was wrong. I didn't know the Lord at that point either…and I fell in love—no, I *believed* I was in love with Zane. And, you know how we've talked about you being abstinent until you fall in love and get married." He nodded. She knew he hated talking about this, but she'd insisted. Her mother had made the mistake. Because of her history, she'd made it a priority to be honest and open about relationships. Until now, he hadn't known her frankness came from her own experience. Looking at him, she paused. How could she tell him that she'd made a mistake but that he was a blessing at the same time?

Keep going.

"Max. What I'm trying to tell you is that Zane is your father." She said the words and the entire world came to a screeching halt. There was no sound. There was nothing but the fear that she'd just lost the most precious thing in her life. Her son's trust.

"Wait, my dad isn't…" He paused on David's name. She'd gotten him away from David early enough and Max had stopped calling David his dad long ago. Max didn't talk about him and despised the fact that he'd beaten her. Oh, how she'd longed to erase David's name from Max's birth certificate and to tell Max the truth.

"No, he isn't."

Max bolted from the chair, his fists at his side as he glared at her. "All these *years*—you knew! All this time and you never said nothin'. And him—Zane, he knew, too, and he's just now coming around. What kind of dad—"

"No." Rose stood, too, and tried to lay her hand on his arm, but he shrugged her off and moved away. She blinked back scalding tears. "Zane didn't know. I never told him. I haven't told him yet."

Max was red with anger and Rose suspected the need to cry, also. Fury raged in his eyes and *she'd* put it there. Her heart was breaking.

"He doesn't know? All this time, living in shelters—in our car—and he was out there all along. And you didn't tell either one of us?"

The accusing words tore at her heart. "I'm sorry—"

"How could you *do* that?" he cried, then turned and raced into the woods.

Chapter Six

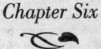

Zane stopped in front of Rose's house just as she came hurrying out of the woods. She was still pale and didn't look happy to see him. So be it. She'd get no sympathy from him. He wanted answers and he wanted them now. He'd tried to stay away, to calm down before coming here, but one look at her and his anger reappeared front and center.

He slammed his truck door while looking around for Max. He didn't see him. That was good for the moment.

"Why didn't you tell me?" he snapped, striding toward her, meeting her in the center of the yard.

"Tell you?" she snapped back, glaring up at him. "*You* left *me*. Remember? Walked away from me like I meant n-nothing to you. Why would I tell you anything? And how dare you, Zane Cantrell, judge *my* motives!"

Like I meant nothing. The words stung but he wasn't in the mood for feeling sympathy. Or guilt. "I left you because I was doing what I thought was best for your safety. That was my job. Had I known about Max I would have come back."

"And that was the last thing I wanted." The words were bitter. "I would never have used Max as a reason to bring you back. For all I know you might have slept with all of the women you were assigned to watch over."

The words struck him like a slap. "I'd *never* done that before," he said in a low voice of barely refrained anger. He'd loved this woman.

"I don't believe you."

"Fine. Believe what you want, but you had no right to keep Max from me. You stole fourteen years with my son from me. Years I will never get back. Doesn't that bother you in the least?"

She sucked in a heavy breath; her shoulders rose with the power of it but she didn't say anything. As if she felt like she didn't have to. Well, he was going to make her understand that from now on she would have to answer to everything that pertained to their son.

"You say you did what you thought was best for our son. How could the best be living on the run? Never having a place to call your own? I could have helped you."

Her eyes narrowed. "You taught me to live that way."

"I did no such thing. Giving you a new identity in a town, with a roof over your head, is a lot different than living in a succession of battered women's shelters. How could you choose to live the way you did when all you had to do was contact me? What kind of mother would do that to her son when she had other options?"

She paled and he almost felt bad. Almost. He was too angry.

"You walked away. You weren't an option."

"I am now. And you can bet I'll be getting to know my son. My lawyer will see to that. I want my rights as a parent." That scared her; he could see it written all over her, from the slumped shoulders to the trembling hand that she pressed to her heart. Good.

"I—I wouldn't stop that."

He ignored the way her wobbly words tore at his heart. How could he feel anything for her after this betrayal? "I don't really care if you would or wouldn't. I passed the point of caring what you would or wouldn't want the minute I saw my son."

His threat hit its mark and he watched her sink onto an old bench. She looked as if her world was spinning. Let it spin. He was working off shock now so let her see what it felt like.

Of course, he wouldn't do anything at this point to prevent Max from forming a relationship with him. That was exactly what keeping Max away from her would do. But she didn't have to know that…he had to have time to weigh all of his options.

Looking at her, his anger intensified—there was a part of him that wanted to pull her into his arms and tell her not to worry, that everything would be okay. It was unbelievable to him that he could feel that. Still, those feelings were overshadowed by the part of him that despised her for what she'd done.

"Where is he?" He wanted to see Max. Talk to him again. This time knowing he was conversing with his son. She blinked rapidly and he knew she was fighting tears. He didn't care. "You can't stop me from seeing him."

"I'm not. It's just…" Her gaze flew toward the trees and then back to Zane. She looked paler than before. "I told him about you a few hours ago."

"And how did he take it?"

"He's upset. Understandably. Very angry." Her voice cracked and she blinked hard, brushing the back of her hand across her cheek when a tear escaped. "How do you think he feels? His mother betrayed him."

Zane had to harden his heart against the agony he saw in her face and heard in her words. She'd caused this. "Does he think I abandoned him, too?"

She looked at the ground. "I explained that you didn't know. But I couldn't explain why you left in the first place."

He yanked his hat off his head and slapped it against his thigh. "Where is he?" Zane had to talk to him. Had to explain. Had to try to fix this.

"He likes to be alone when he's upset…but he ran off over three hours ago and hasn't come back."

"Three hours!" he roared. "And you haven't called anyone?" Zane hated the thought of Max out there in those woods upset, angry and alone.

"I was about to call for some help."

"You should have called me immediately. Aren't you worried?" The words were meant to cut. How many times over the years had his son needed him and he hadn't been there?

"How dare you insinuate that I'm not worried! Of course I'm worried sick. It's not like him. But—"

Zane shook his head and stormed toward the trees he'd seen her coming from when he arrived. His disgust with her was like a living thing between them as she hurried to catch up to him. He didn't care how mad or angry she was with him. All he wanted was to find Max and make sure he was okay. He was seized with a sense of urgency that seared him almost to the point of helplessness. Was this how a parent felt? He forced down the panic with iron determination. Max was fourteen.

"He's always gone off to be alone when he has something bothering him. But he always comes back within a couple of hours."

Her words were breathless as she tried to keep up with him. He didn't slow down as he scanned the trail and the bushes for signs, anything that might show which way he'd gone.

"I've learned to give him the space he needs. But this situation isn't like losing a ball or doing badly on a test. This has been a shock to him."

Irritation flared. "Which way did you check earlier?"

She nodded right, so he strode left off the path. What would he say to Max when he found him? The question unnerved him as he pushed forward through the scattered pine and scrub trees. It was quickly apparent to him that Max had come this way and Zane followed the signs, a broken branch here and trampled leaves there. Rose was quiet as she trailed him, maybe she was praying…Zane was. Somewhere in the seconds between panic and anger he'd begun to pray that God would protect his son and that He would give Zane the words and the wisdom to fix the mess they were in. Because he was out of his element.

There was no way he could do this on his own.

Deputy Cantrell was his dad! Max had been letting the knowledge sink in for hours now. All his life he hadn't actually known his dad. The man who he thought was his father all this time wasn't. That fact alone relieved him of so much bottled-up anger that it was unreal. The no-good jerk!

His mom didn't know it, but Max had always promised himself that when he was old enough, he'd go find David Kimp and tell him exactly what he thought of him. He was glad his mom had taken back her maiden name so he didn't have to go around wearing the name of a rotten coward. Any man who'd beat up on a woman wasn't nobody to be proud of, that was for sure.

Max wondered if Zane's name was on his birth certificate. What did it say? Man, he couldn't believe his mom had *lied* to him.

All this time she'd kept all these secrets.

He slapped his hands to his thighs and from where he sat, cross-legged on his favorite rock, he stared out across the valley. He loved this place. Mule Hollow had all sorts of terrain. Flatland littered with rocks and cacti and deep valleys that were like places he'd only seen in movies and magazines before he came here. This was one of those places. Not like Los Angeles, where he'd always felt hemmed in. Out here he felt free and happy, especially sitting here in his thinking spot—his dreaming spot.

He'd gone from furious to calm to excited in a matter of minutes. Sure he'd been mad at his mom but he knew her…knew that all she'd ever tried to do was protect him and find a better life for him. He wasn't a kid anymore. He'd considered himself a man for a lot longer than the adults had and he figured this was his moment to step up and prove what he was made of. All this time he'd been trying to prove he wasn't like his dad—like David. He'd thought he had his blood running through his veins and it had killed him… But that wasn't so.

He grinned. He couldn't help it—he had a *dad!* A hero dad.

Zane hadn't been around, but he hadn't known he had a son. If he had known he *would* have been around—he was a Texas Ranger after all. Just thinking about the possibilities made Max want to jump up and down like a little kid.

He had a Texas Ranger dad!

It just couldn't get any better than that.

All these years he and his mom had wandered around, hiding. They'd even lived in their car for a few weeks, though he didn't really remember it. And all this time he'd been ashamed because his dad was an embarrassment to the human race—but that hadn't been the truth. His mom had lied to him all this time.

Max thought about that, and, yeah, it bothered him, but he decided he didn't care. What he cared about was that he had a dad who was a hero. *A hero!*

He bolted up, unable to keep all the feelings inside anymore. He jumped in the air and let out a yell, pumping his fist. Life just could not get *any* better than this!

The only thing that would have been better was if they'd been a family together all that time. The idea froze him in his tracks.

What if…what if there was a way for that to happen *now?*

Max's heart started pounding like a thousand stampeding horses. Ever since he and his mom had moved to Mule Hollow, he'd been praying she'd marry a good cowboy. He'd seen how happy all the ladies were who'd gotten married and he wanted that for his mom. But this, this was way better.

He started walking. It was time to go home because he had things to do. Plans to make. Big plans!

He knew just the people to help him, too. The idea

made him walk faster, pushing tree limbs out of his way as he went.

He lived in Mule Hollow with a bunch of women who made happily-ever-after happen all the time.

You betcha that's what they did! And now, it was his mom and dad's turn at a happily-ever-after…he could hardly wait.

He was going to make this happen.

"Ohhh!" Rose cried when she tripped on some underbrush and landed on her hands and knees. She'd been tramping through the woods after Zane for the past fifteen minutes. The man had become a raging bear storming through the trees and her short legs just couldn't match his pace.

"Are you hurt?" he asked, spinning toward her, the tone more a demand than inquiry.

"No," she snapped, using the moment on her knees to take a deep breath. She was so worried about Max she didn't know what to do. Add Zane on top of that and the fear that he might file for custody, and she was a wreck. He'd mentioned his lawyer.

"Are you sure?" he asked, startling her by stooping down in front of her. His expression was grim and his anger at her still very evident, but no one would ever say Zane Cantrell didn't come to their rescue. Oh, no, the man was Mr. Rescue all the way.

"Let me look at your hands," he said, and before she had time to react, he grabbed both her wrists and turned her palms up.

"No, I'm fine," she said, jerking her hands only to have his grip tighten and hold her still. The last thing she wanted was for him to touch her. The man's touch did things to her system that she didn't welcome. Even now, while she was so angry with him she could slap him, her heart was pounding. From rage, she told herself, but she was afraid it was a lie. It was infuriating!

"I don't need your help," she ground out through clenched teeth.

"Yeah, you've made that obvious. Now hold still," he demanded, and bent his head to examine her palms.

They were too close and she was not comfortable at all. Rose tugged her hands again, which only caused him to shoot her a glare.

"I'm telling you to hold still, Rose. I mean it. Your hands are scraped."

Needing to be free from his touch, she wrenched her hands away and stood up. "What we need to do is find my son," she snapped, and started through the woods again calling Max's name.

Her life had turned back into a nightmare and she felt powerless to fix it.

What if he tried to get custody?

She was a good mother. But she was terrified. Would a judge look unsympathetically on the fact that she'd chosen to live in shelters rather than give her son the chance to have a better life with his dad? Max was fourteen. She was almost certain he would be given a choice of which parent he wanted to live with, but the thought of him being put in that situation pained Rose.

And as angry as he was at her right now, if he were given the choice, he might choose Zane. She broke into a cold sweat at the thought. She was literally sick with second-guessing her choices. Every conceivable bad scenario of her life was racing through her mind.

Where was he? She called his name again. Zane

echoed it from half a foot behind her. The man was practically breathing down her neck!

When Max suddenly came into view, her heart leaped with joy and relief. *Thank You, God.*

"Hey," he said, as if nothing was amiss. He gazed at Zane, clearly surprised to see him with her. "What's up?" he asked with a grin.

"'What's up?'" she snapped. "What kind of question is that, young man? You had me worried sick! Where have you been?"

"I've been sitting on a rock thinking and letting everything sink in. I'm sorry, Mom. Really. But you have to admit you gave me a hunk of stuff to think about." His attention switched back to Zane.

She realized, surprisingly, that he wasn't mad. Or upset. Instead, he was clearly infatuated with Zane. She was totally confused. Her son had a certain way of processing things—he'd always met things head-on after he mulled them over. As he'd matured, this trait had grown stronger. Still, he'd been so angry when he'd stormed off, and this was so much bigger than anything he'd faced before, that the grin on his face was unexpected. It worried her.

"So, I hear you're my dad," he said, shocking her further.

Surprise flickered in Zane's eyes, but he hid it well. His quick nod belied the confusion she knew he must be feeling. As he held Max's gaze with sincerity, Rose's heart caught. Once upon a time, she'd looked into Zane's eyes and believed that sincerity with her whole heart. She looked away and inhaled slowly. There was no one else who could look at her and make her believe she could jump tall buildings in a single bound. It was a dangerous thing and scared her for her son…because it only meant she'd fallen that much further when she realized Zane's heart hadn't been as steadfast as his eyes would have one believe.

She prayed he wouldn't hurt Max like he'd hurt her. She would do whatever it took to prevent that from happening, but for now, there was nothing she could do except watch in wonder as her son had his first conversation with his dad.

"Yes, I'm your dad. I didn't know," he said. "But your mom had her reasons for not telling me."

Zane wasn't going to try to use her actions against her with Max. Relief surged though her. She'd been afraid he might, but then, this was the most gracious way to handle it for both of them and in Max's best interest. She gave Zane a grateful nod when he glanced her way.

"Mom told me you watched over her when she was in the witness protection program. That's so cool."

"It was my job. Your mother was very brave to do what she did."

Rose felt a tinge of regret at another reminder that looking out for her had been merely a job to Zane. She knew it was illogical after all this time for it to hurt, but it did.

Max grinned at her and she wanted to scream at him to stop. He had to be hurting inside but was pretending everything was okay. He'd just met his dad. His mom had lied to him. And yet he stood here grinning and looking at her like she hadn't done anything wrong.

"Mom is the bravest woman I know."

His words broke her. Blinking back tears, Rose felt her heart shatter. She wasn't brave at all. She was a hypocrite. All these years, she'd hidden from the most important thing in the world…the truth.

She spun and started toward the house, not wanting him or Zane to see the tears. "Let's go home," she managed and walked blindly back the way they'd come.

Chapter Seven

"So, how are you?"

Rose gave her boss, Ashby, a "What do you think?" look as she brought an armload of clothes out of the dressing room of Ashby's Treasures. "It is an *impossible* situation."

"I still can't get over you being in the witness protection program. And that Zane is Max's dad. That kid is so proud. He's told everyone."

All morning Rose wondered when Ashby would notice the elephant in the room. "I've misled everyone. Max is the best thing that ever happened to me. But I just couldn't chance opening up my past. I hope no one thinks less of me."

"You know none of us think less of you. We love you."

"I know," Rose sighed. "I'm ashamed I even said that. I'm just not thinking straight. What am I going to do, Ashby? Everything is so messed up."

Ashby patted the stool in front of her and Rose left the dresses on a display table and sat down.

"I keep getting the feeling that there's still something between the two of you. Is there?" Ashby asked.

"Not if he was the last man on the planet," Rose groaned. "The man lied to me, *abandoned* me when I needed him most." She sprang up from the stool and started pacing, for no reason other than it kept her from kicking something. It was a sensation she'd been fighting ever since watching Zane and Max bonding last night. "And if that isn't enough, after all these years he's tracked me down in the one place I've been happy."

"But that's my question," Ashby said. "If he didn't know about Max, then why exactly did he do that?"

Rose swung toward Ashby. "Because he feels guilty, that's why. But after all these years it's a little too late for that." And having to tell Max the truth only cemented that.

"Are you sure?"

"Yes, I'm sure. I—I despise the man," Rose insisted. "And believe me, after yesterday, the feeling is mutual. He was off-the-charts angry at me for not telling him about Max."

"Rose, honey… You know I love you and wouldn't want to hurt you, but don't you think his feelings are understandable?"

"He walked away from me. Left me pregnant and alone—"

"But you said yourself that he didn't know you were pregnant."

"Right," she sighed. This was exactly how she feared a judge would look at it. "But surely he had to know I was wearing my heart on my sleeve where he was concerned. And he left me there."

"What exactly happened? Do you want to talk about it?"

Rose needed to talk and she'd already felt bad about

not telling Ashby long ago. "When I entered the program, I trusted him. I felt so alone and scared. He made me feel safe… Foolishly, I let my guard down. I won't lie to you. I loved him then and I thought he loved me. It was just a bad situation all around. I found out how wrong I was when someone tried to shoot me. Zane got me out of the safe house where the attack took place and into another one." She hardened her heart against the emotions just thinking about the experience caused her. "And then he was gone the next morning. No explanation. Just gone." She paused as the devastation she'd felt resurfaced. Taking a breath, she told Ashby how she'd been so afraid the morning after the attack when she walked into the kitchen and found an unfamiliar Texas Ranger pouring himself a cup of coffee. She'd been terrified, not to mention heartbroken.

She took a breath. "I don't know how exactly I made it through the next few months. They were horrible. I found out I was pregnant right before I testified against the man who wanted me dead. Then I was whisked away into a new life in the program only to have the murderer be killed in jail. That was six weeks altogether and the next thing I knew I was released from the program and expected to resume life as if nothing had happened."

Ashby looked as dazed by the information as Rose had felt living it. "I can hardly believe it," she said. "Did they know you were expecting?"

"No. I couldn't believe it myself, so I couldn't bring myself to tell anyone."

"So what did you do then? You must have been so lost."

"Yes. That's a perfect word for how I felt. My grandmother was dead and I really didn't have anything to come home to… And I just couldn't deal with the questions that might be asked by everyone, so I stayed in L.A. and got a job as a receptionist at an import business. And that's when I met David." She shook her head.

"That is amazing," Ashby said, coming to stand beside her. "You are so strong."

"Now I am. But then I wasn't. I married a man because I was afraid of being alone and pregnant and he abused me. I should never have let myself get into such a vulnerable position in the first place."

"I'm so sorry," Ashby said.

Rose took a deep breath and exhaled slowly. "Me, too," she said finally.

"Do you think Zane knows about what David did?"

"He found out when he decided to look me up again," Rose answered bitterly.

"I bet he felt terrible when he found out."

Rose gaped at her friend. "Don't feel bad for him."

Ashby looked sheepish. "I'm sorry. But I do. You and Zane were both in an impossible situation. Maybe you should give yourself and him a break."

A break! She'd like to break something, all right. But give him a break? No way.

"Rose, don't look at me like that. He said he left because he was trying to protect you. He clearly thought he was doing the right thing and that was it. Maybe he's telling the truth. What if you opened your heart and gave him a second chance? It is amazing what you've gone through together. This time you can really get to know each other under normal circumstances. Maybe God's giving you a chance to get it right this time."

Rose stared at Ashby. "Get it right?"

Ashby looked like she was talking to a kindergartner. "Do I have to spell it out?"

"Please do."

"What if God meant for you two to be together all along, but you two put the cart before the horse, so to speak. And maybe it was because you were in such a tense situation that things got out of hand. Don't you think God forgives mistakes and gives second chances?"

Rose nodded. "Yes, I do. But in this situation, it isn't God's ability to forgive that's in question. It's mine."

"Rose, I can't believe you said that. You're the first person who would have told me to trust God. Actually, you *are* the person who told me to trust the Lord when I was struggling with opening my heart to Dan."

Rose looked at the ground. "Oh, Ashby, I know. I feel mean and at odds with everything right now. I'm so ashamed."

Ashby chuckled, leaned forward and hugged her. "Honey, everyone gets there at some point. It just means you need some extra time on your knees with the Lord. He will help you sort it all out."

Rose knew this might be true, but at the moment she just couldn't see how.

"You want us to help you make your mom and Zane fall in love?"

Max nodded at Norma Sue. He'd ridden his bike the three miles between home and the women's shelter where he and his mom used to live. This shelter was different, not only because it was located on Sheriff Brady's ranch, but also because Dottie had opened a candy store in town where she taught all the ladies how

to make candy and run a business, too. Since Dottie
was getting ready to have her baby any day, that meant
the candy store was shorthanded and Norma Sue,
Esther Mae and Adela were babysitting the young
kids while their moms all worked. The older ladies
usually helped out at different times, not all coming
out to the shelter at the same time to watch the kids.
But yesterday he heard his mom and Miss Adela
talking about how the three of them were using the
time to make a baby quilt for Dottie. He'd been trying
to figure out a way to get their help all week long, so
this was his chance. Especially since it was his mom's
Saturday to work at the dress store. She wouldn't
know he'd talked to them.

He still couldn't believe Zane Cantrell was his dad
or that his mom had met him while she was in the
witness protection program—that was just plain cool.
He'd told his friends first thing. By now everyone in
town knew Zane was his dad. It kinda made Max want
to stand taller when he walked down the streets.

"Yeah, I want y'all to do that matchmaking stuff on
my mom and my dad." He grinned. Sheri, the nail tech
down at Heavenly Inspiration hair salon, called these
three the matchmaking posse and he liked the sound
of that. They could help him rope his mom and dad
into a wedding. "Everybody knows that's what y'all
do. You've helped match up almost the entire town, so
why not my mom and dad?"

Norma Sue laid her hand on her wiry gray head and
stared at him like he had horns. The other two were
silent, too. Maybe they hadn't had anyone actually *ask*
for their help and didn't exactly know how to take it.

"I figure maybe y'all like coming up with who you
want to match up all by yourselves. The thing is, I've

made up my mind about this and I'm not going to quit until y'all help me." His mom would tan his hide if she heard him talking like that, since it sounded kind of rude. But a guy had to be firm about important things.

"If that ain't the cutest thing!" Esther Mae squealed suddenly, shattering the silence. "This is going to be so fun!"

Max laughed, but stopped when Norma Sue held up a hand.

"Hold on, Esther Mae," she snapped. "Adela, what do you think?"

Max hadn't ever known his grandmothers, so these ladies were the closest thing he had to that. He had pretended ever since coming here that they were his family. Esther Mae was the funny grandmother. She was always squealing and laughing—and she had short red hair. Norma Sue was the grandma who took charge and made things happen. Yet she didn't look too sure about his idea. He looked at Miss Adela. She was the gentle one. He was always afraid he was going to hurt her when he hugged her because she looked so delicate. Now, he prayed she would think he had a great idea. When smiled, her blue eyes lit up like Christmas lights.

"Well," she said. "If this child wants us to help him get his mother and dad together we have to help him."

"Yes! So what do we do?" he asked.

Norma Sue crossed her arms and shook her head. "I'm not sure we're doing the right thing here. But there were some sparks flying at church last Sunday. I say all we have to do is get them together as often as possible. If God's got a hand in this union, they'll do most of the work themselves."

"When love is involved, they always do," Esther Mae added.

Max frowned. "But what if there isn't? My mom doesn't act like she wants anything to do with Zane. And, well, he tries to hide it from me, but I think my dad is kinda mad at my mom. What if we need to *make* them fall in love?"

"Max," Adela said. "If there's no love there then we don't want them together. And neither do you, dear."

He didn't like the sound of that. "They'll love each other. I know it."

"Even if they don't love each other, they love you, Max." Norma Sue said.

The other two nodded their heads.

"You aren't angry over all of this in some way, are you?" Adela asked.

He sat on the porch banister and looked out at the laughing little boys playing on the swings and sighed. "I got angry at first," he admitted. "But, well, then I got to thinking about it and all the anger just went away. I'm trusting God on this. I've been through a lot in my life and He's always been there for me. Like He's been there for those little guys. I mean, He brought us all here, didn't He? To me, that was God having my back."

"Oh," Esther Mae gasped, patting her eyes with her napkin. "I just want to squeeze you so tight. Goodness, your momma raised you right. She would be so proud of you."

Max wasn't so sure about that. But a man had to do what a man had to do when it came to what was best for his family. Right?

Chapter Eight

Rose was in full work gear when the loud purr of an engine signaled someone was heading down their drive. She poked her head out of the barn door then swung back into the shadows.

Zane. "Oh, for goodness' sake!" she muttered.

When she'd talked to Ashby, she'd just thought he'd invaded her space…but in these short few days the man was *everywhere!* He had truly taken over her life and didn't even know it. He was all Max talked about, all the town talked about—Mr. Good Samaritan in the flesh! But that wasn't the worst part. He was all she thought about—and not in a good way. Well, not exactly in a good way. How could she still be so attracted to a man who had treated her so badly? It was upsetting. From the window of the dress store she saw him coming and going up and down Main Street and there was just no denying that she found herself watching for him. It was humiliating.

And then there was Ashby reminding her she needed to get on her knees! Give him another chance.

How could her friends so easily take Zane's side anyway?

She knew what it was. It was the same reason she'd so readily given her trust over to the man in the first place. He looked the part. He was the living, breathing epitome of a heroic Texas Ranger. Those strong, weathered features, those straight, almost black eyebrows over his beautiful eyes. Eyes that were so sharp they seemed to look right through you. Not to mention he was as tall and sturdy-looking as an oak. She rubbed her forehead and took a deep breath, trying to calm the agitation strumming through her. It was all physical...this attraction. She'd learned what substance she'd believed he had wasn't really there. So how could she still feel drawn to the man? God was punishing her for her weakness. It was the only thing she could figure out. So be it. It bothered her no end that he was the only man she'd ever encountered who affected her so profoundly.

She breathed in slowly and with no other alternative she made her feet move and walk her out of the barn to stand beside Max—who was beaming like Las Vegas neon.

"Look, Mom, I invited Dad to help us today. Isn't that great?"

Dad—where had that come from? Max had given over to this so quickly it was heart-wrenching. "Sure," she managed, stilling her emotions, her gaze drawn to the truck just as Zane stepped to the ground and closed the door. To her dismay, he smiled, and her heart did that aggravating free fall. She scowled at him, racked with frustration at her reaction to him and the fact that he was here in her yard.

In her life.

To see his son.

The little voice of reason reprimanded her and she closed her eyes for a second. He was here for Max. And for Max's sake, she could rein in her emotions and at least try to be civil.

"Mom's got on her tuna-picking clothes," Max stated as soon as Zane reached them.

True, dressed like she was, she looked like the Creature from the Black Lagoon, but she was at a loss as to why Max would feel he needed to explain her appearance to Zane. She tried not to appear as if it bothered her too much but her brow lifted of its own accord when she looked at him.

He gave her a teasing grin while at the same time taking in her outfit with open confusion. "You think you have *tuna* in your pond?"

Max snorted with laughter. "No, Dad. Tuna is what the prickly pear fruit is called."

"Seriously?" Zane asked.

"Yeah—weird but true," Max informed him. "The botanical name means American Indian fig. Or—" he shrugged "—tuna, as it is most commonly called."

Zane looked impressed. "You know your stuff."

Unexpectedly, Rose's heart warmed at the way Zane looked at their son.

Max beamed in her direction. "Mom taught me everything I know. Even how to dress when I pick the tuna."

She'd almost forgotten how ridiculous she looked with her gear on until Zane let his gaze scan over her.

"So is *this* how you dress?" he asked.

"Yes. It's for protection," she snapped, tugging at her bandana and all too aware of her goggles.

"Well, I'm relieved." Zane looked back at Max. "For a minute there, with those goggles on, I figured she might be going for a swim in the pond looking for those tunas."

Max hooted. "*Mom* wouldn't swim in the pond for a million bucks! The goggles are to protect her eyes from the prickly pear's stickers. She makes me wear them, too—if I don't, then I can't be a partner."

"Is that so?" Zane asked, laughing huskily.

The sound was disconcerting in an all-too-familiar way that sent her pulse skittering.

"Your mom sounds like a smart woman," Zane said, his eyes warm.

"Well, boys," Rose said, snapping herself out of her unbelievable lapse in judgment. She gave Zane a chilly glare. "This *smart* woman has work to do." And she did! "You two have fun, or whatever." She stepped back and Zane smiled, as if he knew what she was thinking. "Um, I'll be out there," she said, and tore her eyes away from him.

Shoulders back, she made herself walk calmly across the yard and into the cactus field. Why had he been looking at her like that? Why had she so easily responded to it? It was humiliating. It really was.

Hidden from view by a large cactus, she jerked her goggles over her eyes. She wanted to scream with frustration, but that wouldn't do at all. Instead she went to work.

Max's laughter drifted to her. Despite herself she looked in his direction. Her chest tightened and tears sprang to her eyes, blurring her vision. She didn't know if the tears were because of seeing Max with his dad and enjoying himself or if it was because she was getting a glimpse of how things could have been for them. How she'd first dreamed of life with Zane... How they could have been as a family.

Or maybe she was crying because looking at Zane just made her *crazy* frustrated, and so angry she wanted to scream!

"Bingo," she growled, snatching a tuna with the tongs and ripping it from its perch. The overripe fruit immediately rewarded her by splattering deep magenta mush all over her shirt and face!

Max had the job of scorching the thistles off the fruit down to a fine science with the torch and tongs. When he finished he held a smooth tuna up for Zane's inspection.

"Cool, huh?" He beamed. "Now it's edible. Do you know that there were times when this was about the only thing the Indians had to eat during this season? The fields of cacti stretched for miles and all sorts of different tribes would set up camp near them."

"I didn't realize it was that much of a food source."

"It's some good stuff. Helps with burns, too."

"I'm impressed, son."

"Thanks, *Dad,*" Max said, flashing a Cantrell smile before turning serious. "I'm going to make a success of this. Me and *Mom.*"

Zane nodded, not sure how to take Max's clear flag that there was a solidarity that he shared with his mom that he could never share with him. It wasn't a good feeling, even though he was still having a hard time wrapping his head around the fact that this was his son. He'd come to Mule Hollow to try to see if there could be any hope of a life with Rose and now Max was in the picture, too. All these years she'd kept him away from this amazing kid. A kid who, if Zane understood right, had just let it be known that to have a real, lasting relationship with him would require Zane to get along with Rose. A tall order after what she'd done—the fact that he'd just carried on an almost flirtatious conversation with her was startling.

"So, you and my mom must have really liked each other?"

Zane wasn't sure where the conversation was heading and tried to hide some of his surprise. But even with the goggles Max wore, his piercing scrutiny dug deep.

Zane glanced toward Rose, half hidden from view as she plucked the fruit from the cactus. His gut tightened. Despite the distance he saw anger in the force with which she was working. After all the deceit, he didn't know what he was feeling for her, but he knew the only answer he could give Max was an honest one.

"Yes, I liked your mother very much. I thought she was the bravest, most honorable young woman I'd ever met." *Thought.*

Max laid his torch down, tugged his goggles up to rest on his forehead. "You aren't going to hold this against her, are you?"

Fatherly pride swelled through Zane. Max was a young man who seemed to meet challenge head-on. And, as torn as he was with what was going on inside of him where Rose was concerned, Zane knew this trait came from the way she'd raised Max.

"She only did what she thought was right," Max continued. "She said you left the day after someone tried to kill her. Why'd you do that? You ran out on her when she needed you most."

Zane fought the urge to loosen his collar—a collar that was already unbuttoned. The kid had guts. "You're right. I messed up. I never planned on what

happened between us. I'm not proud of what I did."
The fact that his first serious conversation with his son
was *this* topic was punishment in and of itself for past
sins. How did he talk about this?

"Look, I'm still a kid to most people. But most
folks don't realize everything me and Mom have been
through. My mom has always been up front with me
early on about how important it is to wait for the right
person, *marry* her and experience things the way God
intended it to be."

Zane was successfully chastised. But Max wasn't
through with him.

"And," he continued, "now that I know the truth
about myself, I get it more than ever why Mom was
so straight with me. She didn't want me messing up
like she did. She doesn't want me messing up some
girl's life and leaving her like you left Mom."

Shame settled in the pit of Zane's gut. He'd felt it
and guilt over the years about letting his relationship
with Rose get personal. But never had he felt it so
acutely. The fact that he hadn't known she was expecting his child didn't matter. The fact was as her protector and as the man who'd cared for her, he'd let her
down in every sense of the word, so he kept silent now.
His son deserved to have his say.

"You ran out on her. That was pretty heartless.
You're a Texas Ranger. You're supposed to be a *real*
man. And my mom taught me that a real man stands
up for his responsibility."

Talk about laying it out there! Zane felt like he was
the kid and Max the father. "I left because I put your
mom at risk. I blamed myself for almost losing her. I
was distracted by my feelings for her when the shooter
came after her. I should have seen him, sensed him

long before I did. I left because I didn't want to take the chance that it would happen again."

His gut twisted even now, thinking back to the moment he'd realized Rose had gone outside the safe house. The fact that she'd disobeyed his direct order was not consolation to him. If he'd kept his distance like he'd been trained to do, Rose wouldn't have considered going against him. No one ever had before. But he'd let her see a personal side of him, and because of that she'd felt too comfortable and not taken him seriously. The result had been costly. "My job was to keep her safe—no matter what it cost me personally. That meant no matter what I felt for her, if I didn't feel like I was doing my job, then I had to give it up. And that's what I did. Can you, as a man, understand where I'm coming from?" He rubbed his hip as a dull ache radiated through it.

The ache and the remembrance of Rose's brush with death had him thinking about his recent assignment…the one that had brought him on this journey at last. He'd almost lost that witness, too. Almost given his life to protect a small-time thug who'd gone state's evidence against a money-laundering ring. Zane's keen sense of awareness had been what saved the man's life. Zane had already sprang into action before the car busted through the barriers blocking the street. That hadn't been the case with Rose's ambush. That she'd survived the shooting had purely been an act of God and nothing that had to do with him protecting her. He'd not been able to forgive himself for that— if she'd been killed…he couldn't even think about that possibility.

"Sometimes a man has to make sacrifices in order to pay for his mistakes."

Time stretched between them while Max considered his words. "Yes, sir," he said at last. "I think I get it. But you could have told her goodbye. She might not be so mad at you if you'd told her goodbye. And…" He took a long breath. "And she might have gotten in touch with you later and told you about me."

There was only so much about his relationship with Rose that Zane cared to talk to Max about. Some was too deep and just too personal. A nod would have to suffice. He couldn't tell Max that he'd been afraid of waiting until morning. That if he'd tried to tell her goodbye he might not have been strong enough to walk away. It was his sworn duty to keep her safe, not to take advantage of her fragile emotional state. Which was what he'd done.

And that was what he'd been afraid of all these years. That what she'd felt for him had really only been misplaced emotions due to his protector role.

Only after his near-death experience had he finally decided he had to find out. And so he'd come to Mule Hollow to see if what they'd had was real. His second chance had turned into so much more. God had given him a chance to know Max. But his resentment of Rose lingered and with it that undeniable connection that he couldn't shake.

Rose was coming out of the pasture, so he used her approach as a way not to continue the conversation. What could he say?

She moved with the quick grace of a woman who had things to do and places to be. Without preamble, she set the bag on the table near him, her gaze touching his like the quick sting of a wasp before lighting on Max. She had purple juice splattered all over herself, across her goggles, her cheek and down her neck.

"I'm going to go work in the kitchen. If you need me, just call," she told him then strode toward the house.

It was clear that she was tolerating him for Max's sake—just like he was doing.

So why couldn't he pull his gaze from her?

"Sure thing," Max said, not giving away to her that he'd just taken Zane to the mat. He poured some sad-looking fruit out onto the table. *"Mom,"* he said, laughing. "What happened? You *killed* them."

She cringed. "Sorry."

Zane chuckled unexpectedly and drew a pointed look from her. It only made Max's grin widen broadly as she cut those eyes back to him.

"I'll need those as soon as you can get them to me," she said coolly before heading toward the house at a brisk gait.

Max lifted one shoulder. "She gets like that when she has stuff on her mind." He pulled his goggles down and picked up his torch. "I better get a move on."

"Sounds that way." Zane's attention was drawn back toward the house where Rose was removing her equipment. As he watched, she lifted both hands and smoothed her hair as if smoothing the tendrils would smooth her nerves. Unexpectedly, she glanced his way and caught him watching her. She froze, then yanked open the door and stalked inside.

"I better do the same. It's time for me to relieve Brady from duty." He started to go then stopped. "Max, I honestly never meant to hurt your mom."

Max looked somberly at him. "I don't think she knows that."

He squeezed Max's shoulder, wanting to hug him instead, but not sure if now was the right time. "I'll see you later."

"Yes, sir. Later."

Zane's heart felt like lead as he climbed in his truck and headed back toward town. For a man who'd always seen things in black and white, his entire world suddenly seemed washed in gray.

Chapter Nine

"Son, ya got a long row ta hoe," Applegate said the next morning. He lifted a bushy brow. "Ya know that, don't ya?"

Zane frowned into his coffee. "Yes, sir," he said, resigned to the fact that he was about to get plenty of free advice. With his dark mood he probably should have skipped the diner and headed straight to the office, but he wasn't thinking completely straight today.

Sam leaned a hip against the counter. "I know yer upset 'bout her not telling that boy you were his dad, but from what we've been told, that little gal has been through enough to break most folks."

"Yep," Stanley said, talking loud as he and App usually did. "She's a scrapper. It's hard to believe all she's been through. To look at her you'd never believe it."

"So now what?" Applegate boomed, walking over from his forgotten checker game. "You gonna fight fer yourself."

"I'm going to fight for my son," Zane said.

Stanley grunted. "A smart man would fight fer yor *family*."

"I don't have a family." There was still that resentment for what he'd missed—unbelievably strong this morning.

"Oh, phooey!" Applegate exploded. "Don't be a fool. Ya know good and well ya could have a family. If you were a big enough man to get past feelin' sorry fer yourself. You goofed. She goofed. Get over it and on with it."

"Now, App, he don't know that, and neither do you," Sam said. "Rose has a mind of her own. She might not want him after what he did. She might not want to forgive him."

"He could make her want him if he had a mind to," Stanley said, spitting a sunflower seed into the spittoon. "A man's got ta know when ta fight fer what he wants."

Sam glared at him. "And I'm saying he kin fight all he wants, but if Rose don't want him then he ain't got a chance."

Okay, that about did it for him in the advice department. Zane pushed away from the counter. "I'm standing right here, fellas, so would you stop talking about me like I'm not." He'd struggled with his next move all night.

Applegate scowled. "I gotta say, I ain't so sure you're all here. I mean, if you cain't look at that little woman and see a jewel to be won, then thar must be a hole in yer head."

Zane blinked back his sudden irritation. He hadn't known these old guys long, but it was obvious they didn't pull punches. "I guess I have a hole in my head." He slapped a buck on the counter and stalked to the door. He could feel steam boiling and would have welcomed another hole in his head to relieve it.

He wasn't sure about anything at the moment except that he wanted to build a relationship with Max. Sure, he couldn't deny that despite everything there were feelings battling inside of him where Rose was concerned.

Outside, he glared toward the dress store as he walked down the sidewalk to the office. He had too much time on his hands. So far, fixing Mrs. Lovelace's flat had been his most eventful day. He'd had far too much time to dwell on Rose. He hated to wish for something to happen at work, but even something small like another flat tire would give him a momentary reprieve. Maybe then some of the confusion would dissipate.

But this was Mule Hollow, making the odds slim that he'd get any distraction. He kept reminding himself that his job being boring was a good thing for the quiet little town.

To his amazement, the phones started ringing the instant he walked into the office. For starters, a loaded-down cattle hauler had blown a tire, hit a tree and tipped over out on the north side of the county. There were stressed-out cattle running loose up and down the county road. This time they called Prudy's wrecker service to haul away the truck while he and Brady rounded up the cattle until new transportation could be arranged. Needless to say it was a chaotic morning that lasted through lunch. No sooner had they gotten that taken care of than a call came in on a grass fire. As he turned on the lights of the patrol vehicle and fell in line behind Brady's truck, heading toward the fire, he decided maybe wishing for something to take his mind off Rose had been a bad idea.

* * *

Rose had just locked the door for the day when Zane walked across the street and stepped onto the sidewalk. He looked tired and hot as he scooped his hat off and held it limply in one hand. She had never seen him looking rumpled and was startled to see him this way. There was mud caked to his boots and the bottoms of his jeans and his shirt was damp. His short hair clung to his forehead. She'd heard about the cattle truck and the fire.

"Hello, Rose."

"Hi," she acknowledged, and tried hard not to notice how good he looked even rumpled. "Even if I hadn't already heard, I could look at you and tell you've had a busy day."

He gave her a tired smile. "I was under the false assumption that nothing ever happened around here."

"We have our moments. I'm glad the man driving that cattle hauler is okay."

He nodded. "Word spreads quickly around here."

"Surely that doesn't surprise you."

"Not really." They studied each other as an awkward moment of silence ticked by.

"I was just about to leave. Is there something you needed in the store?"

"No."

Okay, then, she thought, and headed toward her car.

"Rose," he said, catching up to her. "I think we need to talk."

"We've been talking." She was evading the issue and she knew it.

"I mean *really* talk. This situation isn't going to fix itself if we don't figure some things out. Peacefully."

"Talk about what? You trying to get custody of my son?" The words were out before she could stop them. Ever since seeing him and Max laughing together yesterday, she'd been fighting off horrible visions of being left out.

"*Our* son," he said firmly.

She stiffened, feeling volatile. "Our son," she amended after a moment.

"We need to find a way to get along. For Max's sake," he added. "Can we do that?"

"For *Max*, I'll do anything." No matter how hard.

"Even talk to a snake like me," he asked, with a hint of a smile.

"Don't push your luck," she warned. "So, what do you suggest?" she asked. He hadn't answered her question about custody, but she was under no illusion. He'd probably avoided answering the question on purpose. If he was going to try to get custody of Max, then maybe her best defense was to let him see her and Max in their home environment.

He surprised her by leaning past her and opening her car door. He smelled of smoke, reminding her that he'd spent all afternoon helping the men in the fire department to stop a grass fire from getting out of control. When his arm brushed hers, she shivered. Even after everything that had happened between them she'd never felt so aware of any man in her life as she did with Zane.

Fool.

"I have a question. I was wondering if you'd mind if I took Max with me to look at a piece of property I'm considering. Haley left the key for me so I could look at it tonight." He held up a key.

Rose's heart skipped a beat. The fact that he wanted Max to help him pick out a new home increased her apprehension. "If he wants to go, I won't stand in his way," she said. What else could she say?

"Thank you. He tells me he wants his own ranch one day."

Jealousy reared its ugly head. Max was sharing his dreams with Zane. It was normal and she had to be glad for Max. He had his dad in his life. She was happy for him. "Yes. He loves everything about life here. Look, I'm going by to see Dottie before I head home, so you can just run out there and pick him up. I'm certain he's getting a new batch of fruit ready for me to cook. Tell him I'll be a little late and to go with you and have a good time."

"I hoped we could talk after I bring him home."

She slid behind the wheel, feeling sick. He draped one arm over the door and bent slightly as he looked down at her. It was too cozy for comfort as she looked up at him. "Sure," she lied.

His gaze softened. "Thank you. Do you think after we get back you could show me some pictures of Max?"

Pictures meant sitting down, thumbing through albums! It meant sharing her past. It meant exposing her and Max's special moments to his scrutiny.

But…how could she deny him? "Yes, certainly. And, um, we can have copies made of anything you want."

"Sounds good to me," he said, looking as if she'd just promised him the world.

Him looking like that was a dangerous thing!

"Be careful," he said, tapping the top of the car before closing her door.

Be careful? Ha! If she were being careful, she would never have invited her worst nightmare to come and sit on the couch and casually thumb through her and Max's life.

Chapter Ten

Rose had just added a cutting board piled high with fruit into one of her four stockpots, when she heard Zane and Max drive up. "Stay calm," she muttered, blotting her damp forehead with the back of her sleeve. "Everything will be okay."

Will it?

How was she supposed to think positively when that voice in her head contributed statements like that?

"Yes, it will." If there was one thing she was good at, it was making lemonade out of lemons. Not just lemons, but rotten lemons. And this was just about as rotten as it got. Zane would not take her son.

He just wouldn't.

If he was as *lovely* a man as the entire town believed—Dottie included—then he wouldn't!

She'd thought Dottie would help her figure out a game plan to keep the man away from her and Max, but she'd been sadly mistaken. Dottie had been curious about how she was handling Zane's arrival, but infatuated, just like Ashby was, with the entire situation.

Everyone's romanticism of her and Zane's past was wearing thin.

"Hey, Mom," Max called, bursting through the doorway.

He came straight to her and gave her a quick hug, which was very much needed.

"Hey yourself, kiddo." She met Zane's gaze over his shoulder.

He'd stopped just inside the doorway and looked as uncomfortable as she felt. It gave Rose a wicked sense of satisfaction—this one-sided stuff was the pits.

"Mom, how about if Dad stays for supper?"

Rose's heart clutched at the title and any pleasure she'd felt disappeared. "Sure," she managed, lifting one corner of her lip in a semblance of a smile, but her hand shook as she reached for the hot pads. It was normal for Max to want Zane to stay. Normal for him to call him Dad.

What do you mean, normal! Nothing about this is normal.

Rose shoved away the hysterical voice. It was just going to have to learn to cope.

Cope. Cope. Cope. She let the word roll through her like a mantra. She could cope. She could cope right along with the best of them. "Why don't you go get washed up," she said to prove it.

"Great," Max said, draping his arm over her shoulders as he was prone to do since he'd grown taller than her. "I'm starved, and after the day Dad's had, I'm sure he is, too." He'd turned them both so they were facing Zane.

Zane was still standing just inside the door and despite her trepidation about the entire situation she felt her heart tug.

Not good. Not good at all. The handsome, hard planes of his face did nothing to dispel the fact that he looked to her like a kid hovering on the outskirts of something he wanted very much to be involved in. Whether she wanted to or not, she felt for him.

"We can look at the pictures you wanted to see of Max after dinner. Please stay."

He shifted his weight from one long, booted leg to the other and nodded. "I'd like that."

"All right!" Max shouted. "I'll be right back."

They both watched him disappear down the hall. Her heart pounded as she turned toward the stove—which seemed to be its normal pace when Zane was around. Of course it could be fear of what he could take from her that drove the pounding…not that long-ago attraction. This was a possibility, she reasoned.

But whatever it was it was trouble.

"Max told me you had a lot of work to do tonight," Zane said, coming to stand near the stove. He leaned forward and peeked at the magenta concoction in the pots. "From the looks of things, I feel bad intruding. I know you must not have time for this."

"No. I have it under control." She glanced at the large pots on the burners and then the other fruit she'd begun to prepare that was waiting its turn. "You can wash up at the sink if you like or follow Max."

"This is fine," he said, picking up the liquid soap and dispensing some into his palm.

The kitchen suddenly seemed too confining, and she wished Max would hurry up. She didn't really know what to say, and so she said nothing. Just found herself staring at Zane's back as he scrubbed his hands at the sink.

"It smells good in here," he said, glancing over his shoulder.

"Sweet," Rose croaked, startled at being caught staring. "Sickeningly so after a while," she blurted out. Snatching up the hot pads, she fumbled to open the oven and seriously considered keeping her head inside—she was so embarrassed.

Thankfully, Max came back into the kitchen moments later as she pulled out the casserole, saving her from having a full-blown breakdown.

"You should see the place Dad is thinking about buying. It's real nice." He explained which property Zane had shown him as he grabbed three plates, then set them on the small table in the corner. The house wasn't big enough to have a dining room and normally the small table was enough. But as Rose set the casserole on a hot pad in the center, she was very aware how cozy one extra place setting made the seating arrangement.

"I know that place," she said. "It has lovely oaks surrounding the house."

"You like it?" Zane leaned a hip against the counter and crossed his arms over his impressive chest.

She nodded. Struggling not to stare, she gave a pot of fruit a stir.

"I liked it, too," he said. "But I'm going to take my time. Hey, put me to work. What can I do?"

"Grab the forks for me," Max said, snagging three glasses. "Since you're leaning on the drawer they're in and nobody else can get to them."

Zane chuckled. "Hey, kid, watch yourself."

Rose laughed. It startled her and she proceeded to reach for the tea and filled the glasses after Max put the ice in them. He and Rose had a little routine they followed getting their nightly dinner on the table. It came from time spent in homes with other families and everyone pitching in to help. There was nothing different about what was going on now…except everything.

Max was chattering away, calling her Mom and Zane Dad. And if Zane felt there was anything uncomfortable about the situation, he didn't act like it anymore. The man suddenly acted right at home—which was the last thing she wanted him to be feeling. Wasn't it?

And it didn't stop with him placing forks and a serving spoon on the table. When they sat down, Max, who always blessed the food for them, passed that honor to Zane. Rose fought off the uneasy feeling that was building inside of her. Max was getting a little too cozy with all of this. But she didn't know what to do about it; she was completely confused.

"So Max tells me you've already got orders for your jelly."

She set her fork on her plate, feeling the familiar tingle of excitement she felt just thinking about her business. She grabbed the topic like a lifeline. "Yes. Several of the specialty shops that stock candy from the candy store have agreed to try my jelly. And I'm selling it at the concession stand that the candy store sets up at The Barn Theater tomorrow evening and Saturday afternoon. Since many of the people who are driving in for the show are tourists they might be interested."

"It's small potatoes right now," Max added. "But we've got plans."

Rose explained. "Max and I are coming up with our business plan so we can get some financing to go larger."

"That's right," Max said. "We're trying to get some sales figures together and have future orders in hand before we approach the bank for a business loan."

Rose felt a bubble of pride expand in her chest as she looked from Max to Zane. He looked just as proud of Max as she felt and their eyes locked as they shared the moment.

"I don't know if you've noticed, but your son is driven to succeed." She said the words *your son* before she even realized it. Zane's eyes widened slightly, letting her know he was as surprised by her use of the term as she was. She knew he took it as acceptance. She, on the other hand, wasn't sure what it was.

"I could tell that," he said. "When we were out looking at my prospective ranch, he was already negotiating the use of a cactus patch on it."

"Max," Rose gasped.

"Hey, Dad's not the only one I'm hitting up. If we want to expand this jelly business, we're going to need more fruit than these few acres can give us. Isn't that right?"

She couldn't help but give in to his charming grin. "I just didn't know you were already getting the ball rolling."

"Mom, believe me, I have everything under control." He looked from her to Zane. "Everything."

She concentrated on her food, finishing it off, then picked up her plate, more than ready to get this evening over with. By bringing Zane into their home, she was unintentionally giving Max false hope that they could become a family. She steadied the butterflies of unease in her stomach and rose a few minutes later. "I guess if we're done we'll go into the living room and look at those pictures."

"That sounds good," Zane said hesitantly. "Are you sure though that another night wouldn't be better since you have so much to do tonight?"

"No. Tonight is fine." She needed to get this over with. Get him out of her house and give him no other reason to enter it again.

"I'll go pull them out," Max offered and left the room.

Rose stared after him. He hated looking at pictures. Then again, it wasn't every day that you got to show your dad your life for the first time. That familiar pang of guilt rang through her at the insight and drove her to keep her composure. She would manage the next hour, because this was for Max.

"I look like a conehead," Max said, leaning over Rose to view the picture Zane had just chuckled at.

"You do not," Rose protested. "You're beautiful."

"You are supposed to say that. You're my mother."

"So you had a pointed head," Zane said, his heart warm with affection as he teased Max. "But I have to agree with your mom. You were a beautiful baby."

"Hey!" Max exclaimed. "I don't call *you* beautiful!"

Zane laughed. "Forgive me. You're about as ugly as a hound dog. How's that?"

"Much better. I've had my cheeks pinched more times than I want to think about."

"It's true," Rose said. "He suffered for his beauty everywhere we lived."

Zane tried to keep the mood lighthearted, but he was struggling. Every picture he looked at of Max and of Rose reminded him that he hadn't been there. Every remark like this one reminded him that they'd lived like vagabonds, moving across the country from shelter to shelter. It also reminded him that Rose had denied him the right to be there for them.

"Hey, I promised Gil I'd call him before nine," Max said, suddenly jumping up from the couch. "Mom, y'all should have some coffee out on the porch or something," he offered amiably before jogging from the room.

The little sneak. Zane hadn't missed the kid's smooth move when they'd come into the living room to look at photos. Despite Rose's protest, Max had worked it out so that she was sitting on the couch between him and Zane. Now she scooted quickly to the spot Max had vacated and let the album slide in between them. Fine with him. He'd been more than aware of her for the past hour. He looked from Max's retreating back to Rose. Embarrassment etched her beautiful face. Yep. He'd found himself drawn to look at her over and over all evening. And he wasn't sure how he felt about that anymore.

"I've taken up too much of your evening," he said, standing, needing to get away from her. He wondered whether she was aware that Max seemed to be trying to get them together.

She stood, too, and headed toward the kitchen, where the air was heavy with sweetness from the cooking fruit. He'd intended to leave straight away but as she moved one large pot from the stove to a hot pad and quickly placed another pot in its place, he found his boots weren't doing any walking. Nope, they were stuck to the floor, even though she hadn't taken Max's suggestion and invited him for coffee on the porch. That alone should have been his prompt to get lost. "I could help if you needed me to."

"Oh? No." She was pouring a colander full of prickly pear into the pot of water and glanced over her shoulder at him. "You don't need to do that. You have work tomorrow so you should go ahead and go."

"You have work tomorrow, too."

She reached for another loaded-down colander. "I can manage."

When she didn't look at him he felt like he'd just been dismissed. There really was nothing else to keep him hanging around. He grabbed his hat from the hat rack. "I guess I'll head out, then. Thanks for showing me the pictures. And for dinner."

She turned, her face flushed from the heat of the stove. "Have a good night." Her voice was soft. Her eyes liquid.

His gut tightened looking at her and he stepped back feeling the screen door behind him. "You, too."

She nodded with a faint smile and turned back to her cooking. Zane really took a step toward her, but whirled and put some distance between them as fast as his bum leg would let him. His mind was reeling— all he was thinking about was how kissable she'd looked. Since learning about Max, he'd gone through a stunning array of emotions from anger to this…this need to hold her. To feel her heart beating next to his.

But she'd lied to him.

He stopped at his truck and slammed his palms to the hood, staring up at the sky. She hadn't lied—she simply hadn't told him he had a son. In her mind she felt her actions were justified since he'd walked away from her…abandoned her. There was no doubt in his mind that if Rose realized he'd been thinking about kissing her, she wouldn't be happy.

And could he blame her?

Chapter Eleven

Brady hadn't been kidding when he said Mule Hollow on a weekend was busy. On Friday evening Zane arrived early to The Barn Theater where he was supposed to "keep the peace." Brady had chuckled as he said the words.

Zane was impressed with the ancient barn that Ross Denton and his wife, Sugar, had converted into an old-fashioned theater. It was a fairly rustic setup, but unique. And from what he'd been told there seemed to be a fair amount of interest from folks who drove in from surrounding areas for the Friday night show or one of the two shows offered on Saturday.

Arriving early, he stood over to the side as everyone went about their jobs setting up. He was there basically to direct parking, so he just tried to stay out of the way until he was needed.

"Zane," Applegate and Stanley called from the loft section where they helped with the sound and lights.

"How's it going, fellas?" He couldn't help smiling. The two hawk-eyed men looked every bit as alert and on the lookout up there as they did sitting at the window seat at Sam's. Nothing was going on here that they didn't see.

"You look like you had a rough night," Applegate hollered.

They didn't miss anything. "You might have a little hearing trouble, but there's nothing wrong with your eyes."

Applegate chortled. "Ain't nothin' wrong with my mind, either. How about yours?"

"Yeah," Stanley asked. "You got thangs figured out yet? Got that hole in your head fixed?"

Several people heard the exchange—they'd have been deaf not to, and they cast curious glances his way.

Not caring to tell the world his troubles, he decided it was time to step outside. App and Stanley's cackles followed him.

They'd been right and they knew it. He'd faced the hard facts last night. Everything she'd done had been in reaction to what he'd done. His fault and his responsibility to fix.

No sooner had he walked out into the sunshine than Norma Sue, Esther Mae and Adela drove up. Norma Sue pulled her big four-door truck to a halt in front of the theater and shoved her door wide open. "Hey, cowboys, can y'all give us a hand? We're delivering fresh chocolates to the concession stand."

She hopped from the truck as Esther Mae stepped from the backseat and Adela from the front.

"Zane, you take this one, will you?"

"Sure." He grabbed a large cooler from the back of the truck and Ross, the theater owner, came over and grabbed the one he was told to get. Adela held open the door of the small food trailer parked a few feet from the entrance of the theater and they deposited their loads, then went back for more.

Two loads down and one to go, Ross left to change into his stage clothes, leaving Zane alone with the *matchmakers*. He'd run into them a few times at Sam's and they made him a little uncomfortable. Always asking him if he'd seen Rose. Just like Max the night before hadn't hidden his agenda too far from the surface, these ladies practically carried banners about him and Rose.

"So, how does it feel to be a dad?" Norma Sue asked as she carried a small cooler beside him. Adela and Esther Mae were inside the trailer getting everything set up for business.

"It's great." Awesome. Unbelievable.

"Bit of a shock, wasn't it?"

"Just a bit. But we're making up for lost time."

She plopped her cooler down on the ground beside the door and hollered inside. "Here's the last of it, girls." Then turned to him, hands on hips. "So, you over being angry and frustrated about what she did?"

Here it came. First the checker players, then the matchmakers. He was quickly coming to realize that Mule Hollow folks were a plainspoken lot.

His first inclination was to tell her it wasn't any of her business, but he didn't. "I'm working on it."

"Good. Smart man. So do you miss bein' a Ranger?"

He tipped his hat back, glad to transfer to another subject. "Yes'm, I do. But I'm adjusting."

"Mule Hollow's a lot quieter than what you're used to, I'm sure."

He nodded.

"I saw some of you men on television last year escorting a witness to a trial. Y'all were loaded down with guns and the man had a black mask over his head to hide his identity. It was something to see. Did you do that kind of thing often?"

His hip sent out a sympathetic twinge. "A few times."

Obviously having been listening in on the conversation Esther Mae stuck her head through the open window of the concession stand. "Is that how they got Rose into the courthouse when she testified?"

"Yes, ma'am."

"Oh, I can only imagine how terrifying that had to be."

"It's not for the faint of heart."

"And our Rose certainly isn't that," Norma Sue added. And as if their words had summoned her, Rose drove over the cattle guard and headed straight for them.

Max was the first out. "Sorry we're a little late. The car had a flat!"

Rose looked flustered. "Max helped me fix it, though. So he's my hero." She popped the trunk and Zane went to help her. What was it with this county and flats?

"You did good, son," he said. "I'll check out your car before you leave here."

Rose looked up at him. "You don't need to do that."

"I do and I will," he said. "I'll also make sure the flat tire is fixed so you'll have a decent spare."

"No, thank you," she said stubbornly.

"Aren't you going to be making deliveries with your jelly all across the county next weekend?" That's what Max had told him.

"Yes, but I'm capable of keeping my car in good repair. And teaching Max."

"The flat came from a nail," Max said, jogging to

stand beside them. "I set the tire beside the porch so you can come out and get me and we can take it to Prudy's Garage and get it fixed."

"I'll do that. And while we're at it we can go over a few other things about car maintenance."

"Sure thing, Dad. Hey, I gotta run, I'm supposed to get the programs from the office and some other stuff before the people start arriving."

"Look," Rose snapped the minute Max was out of earshot. "I can take care of my own car. I don't need you taking charge. I can deal with you wanting to get to know Max, but that's it. Do I make myself clear?"

She pushed her hair back from her face and glared up at him, her cobalt eyes flashing in the sunshine. "Perfectly clear," he said. "I was just trying to help."

"Well, don't."

Puzzled, Zane watched her wrestle a large box of jelly into her arms. His first inclination was to take it from her, but given her current mood she might haul off and clobber him for it. "You look tired," he said instead. Maybe that was it. He'd taken up so much of her time the night before she'd been up extra late working and now she was paying for it…and taking it out on him.

"Gee, thanks," she snapped, and marched past him.

Zane nudged his hat off his forehead and watched her cross the grass toward the concession trailer before he grabbed the other box of jelly and followed her.

"Hi, girls," she said, sliding her box onto the wide counter that spread down the length of the concession trailer. "Better late than never." She gave him a scathing glance as he walked up beside her and set his box in front of Adela.

She smiled at him and plucked a jar from his box. "Oh, this does look wonderful. The color is perfect."

The light caught the color and it glistened translucent and ruby red. Zane didn't know much about jelly except that he liked it on toast and this looked delicious.

"Oh, and look," Esther Mae cooed, peering into the box. "The jar skirts are *so* cute. I love the tiny cactus print."

"Thanks," Rose said. "I think they're cute, too."

Zane was officially in woman territory. "I'm assuming jar skirts are the material on the lid," he said.

Esther giggled. "Well, sure. Don't this look like Norma Sue in a skirt? Short and round."

"Watch it, now," Norma Sue barked, stuffing her fists on her hefty hips. "Looks more like you if you ask me."

Zane grinned. "I get the idea. Only women would put skirts on jars." All the ladies laughed except Rose. They were standing close enough for him to smell her sweet scent and yet it felt like they were oceans apart.

Despite every reason not to, he wanted to pull her into his arms. She looked up at him and took his breath away. He took a hard step back. He tore his gaze away from her and found Norma Sue grinning at him. Esther Mae and Adela were smiling, too.

Rose began unloading jelly from the box. Each jar made a resounding thunk as she slapped it onto the counter. Her skin had a tinge of pink.

"So tell us, Rose," Esther Mae said. Excitement over what he knew they'd all seen in his eyes rang in her voice. "Was it thrilling when Zane was protecting you, or were you terrified? I'd have been terrified."

"Not me," Norma Sue said. "Look at this man." She scanned him with an approving look. "A strapping strong man willing to give his life to protect me—nope, I would have surrendered to his care and not worried at all."

Zane fought off the old guilt her words yanked into the moment.

Adela was watching him carefully. He looked away only to meet Rose's gaze. She knew exactly how incorrect that assessment of his abilities had been when it came to her safety.

"I wasn't scared," she said without hesitation, her eyes holding his. "Zane…is very good at his job."

Her words, forced as they sounded, were like a dunk in ice water. "I've got to get to work," he said, holding back his denial. He tipped his hat and headed toward the open field. She'd lied to the ladies. He knew it and she knew it and it twisted his gut knowing that she'd told those ladies an untruth to protect his reputation. She'd almost been shot because he'd not done his job. But the only way to tell that was to call her a liar and he wasn't going there…at least not in public.

Rose had worked most of the night after Zane left her house. It was either that or waste the night tossing and turning. Having Zane in her house, sitting beside her on the couch looking at photos was hard enough on her. Realizing that Max was trying to push them together had been torment.

There was absolutely no way Zane had missed the way Max had orchestrated their positions on the couch. Nor could he have missed the hopeful looks their son had given them several times through the evening.

Arriving here and finding Zane—looking far too

handsome for anyone's good—was the last thing she needed. Yes, she was irritable. Who wouldn't be?

She'd bit her lip and pulled in her emotions as she watched Zane storm across the pasture. He had a limp. The realization caused an unwanted pain in her heart. The same thing happened when Max got a scrape or a bump. It wasn't the limp, but how he got it.

Instantly her mind flew and she wondered if it was from throwing himself in front of someone, protecting them with his own life. Because she knew without doubt that he'd done it more than a few times during his career. That he would do it without hesitation when it came to protecting whomever he was assigned to.

She remembered his expression moments after her assassination attempt. They were in the garden outside the safe house. He had forbidden her to go out there, said it wasn't safe. But she'd been inside that house for too long and on that day she'd slipped outside just for a moment. When he came out to get her he'd been angry, but she'd kissed him, teasing him for being a worrywart. He was looking at her, smiling when the bullets started.

Rapid fire. They sounded more like taps hitting the window behind her and she didn't realize what she was hearing. But Zane did, throwing her down on the ground beneath him, covering her then rolling her behind a table that he'd flipped on its side somehow. She still couldn't fathom everything that happened in those mere seconds before he practically hauled her inside the house.

Afterward he was barking orders over the phone, and within moments he had her crouching in the floorboard of the SUV as he expertly raced them out of the neighborhood.

He hadn't talked to her the entire time they were on the road. But she could see in his eyes that he was tortured over the whole thing. He was gone the next morning. Until he'd shown up here she hadn't seen him or heard from him again.

Somehow, because of her anger, all these years she'd forgotten how heroic he'd been. How troubled he'd been over what he'd surely viewed as failure on his part.

Forgotten that he would have died for her that day.

She'd forgotten it all the next morning when he'd walked away. All she could think in that moment besides the fact that she was terrified and abandoned was that she'd caused him too much trouble disobeying his orders and he was now done with her.

Thinking about it now, she couldn't move.

"You could fry bacon on the look in his eyes when he's watching you," Esther Mae said.

Rose snapped to attention, shook her head. "He just naturally has an intense look in his eyes. Comes from intimidating all those criminals in his job."

"Shame on you, Rose Vincent." Norma Sue chuckled. "Your eyes are a whole lot younger than ours and you know good and well that the two of you have something going on between you. Everybody sees it."

"There *isn't* anything between us." Anymore. There wasn't and wouldn't be now. Other than Max.

Her tightly wound emotions unraveled as they all studied her, their expressions rapt with intention. The intent to do matchmaking. She knew it well. "Don't," she snapped, looking sternly at each one of them. "Don't. Don't. Don't. I know what's best for me and what you three are thinking is not it. I'm telling you, it isn't. You have no clue what you're doing here."

"You think too much," Norma Sue said.

"That's right," Esther Mae harrumphed. "Just because you have a past together where you, well…" She blushed slightly. "Okay, where you got things out of God's order. Doesn't mean things can't be put back in order."

Rose went back to frantically pulling jelly jars out of the box.

"What about Max?"

Adela's soft words drew Rose to look up. "He's fine."

"Are you sure?"

No. "He and Zane are building a lovely relationship," she said, trying hard not to give away the terror she was feeling at the as yet unspoken threat. She yanked the empty box from the shelf and stepped away from the concession trailer. Cars were starting to stream across the cattle guard, lining up in the pasture waiting for Zane to direct them to the right parking spot. He took her breath away—it was true, no way around it. Everything about the man's physical appearance appealed to her. The way he moved, the way he looked, the way that he just stood there and people took notice. As she stared at him he looked across the distance. The ambient temperature rose by leaps in a flash of those golden eyes. She took a deep breath and turned away.

"Honey, that man is in love with you," Norma Sue said, and her friends echoed her.

Rose groaned. "Stop it. I need to move my car," she said. "When I come back, no more talk about this. Please. No. Don't look like that. I'm serious. Listen, I know you three have the best of intentions, but you have to promise me you'll back off. Max already stands the chance of getting hurt because he wants so much for me and Zane to get together. Your encouragement could make things worse. Do you understand?"

The ladies looked at each other and their rapt expressions faded.

"Promise me you won't encourage my son in this," Rose repeated. She felt a small bit of relief when they nodded. "Okay, good," she said, and then she hurried to her car, where she collapsed in the front seat. Pulling the door closed, she welcomed the silent interior…but even the silence didn't calm the turmoil inside her. Despite what everyone thought, Zane was not in love with her…he was in love with their son.

Chapter Twelve

Rose felt hot and tired as she tromped through the field with four buckets of fruit on Monday. She was working overtime because she had prickly pears ripening too fast to pick. And Max, who had planned to help her today, had awakened that morning and told her that Norma Sue had called to get his help with some baby calves. His desertion was surprising, but she knew that he was good for his promise to make it up to her.

She'd just reached Max's torching table, as he liked to call it, when Zane drove up the lane. If she'd assumed her day couldn't get any worse she'd been wrong.

The day before at church, he'd worn a tan-colored sports coat with his jeans, and the red shirt beneath the tan jacket had set his own burnished skin off to perfection. She couldn't help but notice. She and every other single woman in Mule Hollow would be blind if that were the case.

Max had opted to sit with Zane during the service. He and Gil sometimes sat together in the front pew, so it shouldn't have bothered her so much that he chose to sit with his dad versus her. But it seemed everything about Zane in their lives was bothering her.

That had been yesterday. Today he was dressed casually in a soft chambray long-sleeved shirt that had been washed so much it was as pale as a watercolor sky and the formfitting jeans he wore were almost as pale. And she had absolutely *no* business paying so much attention to his appearance.

The man had never confirmed he was going to try to get custody of Max. That was always on her mind… She shouldn't have been ugly to him on Saturday. She should have been on her best behavior when he was around, but it was impossible. She felt like a firecracker ready to explode when he was near. If he was going to try to take Max then he would have a fight on his hands.

"You look like you could use a hand," he said as he removed his aviator shades, revealing eyes that glinted warmly in the sunlight.

Get a life, Rose!

"No, I'm fine." She wasn't.

"Yeah." He chuckled. "I can see that. You have ten buckets of fruit there. You look exhausted."

"What exactly is it with you always telling me I look exhausted. I'm *not* exhausted. And I said I was fine, so I'm fine."

He raised a brow and took a pair of gloves from his back pocket. "Grumpy, too."

"Wait just a minute—what are you doing?"

He slipped one glove on. "I'm helping you. I should have been here earlier but I ended up having to go into the office for Brady because Dottie had a doctor's appointment."

"Yes, she called and told me she had had a few

pains and that Brady had insisted on taking her in. Wait. What do you mean you would have been here sooner?"

"Max asked me to come help you. He said you could really use a hand. That he had something else he had to get done and felt guilty for leaving you stranded. He said that you were going to be 'working like a dog.' Those were his exact words. How could I refuse?"

Ohhh, that boy! She forced a smile, feeling the strain as she held in a scream of frustration. "I'm perfectly fine. If I'd needed help I would have asked someone."

He cocked a brow and tugged on the other glove. "Yup. Max said you would deny to your dying breath that you needed the help."

"Where does he come up with this stuff?" she grumbled. "We have been set up and I, for one, don't intend to fall for this. I am perfectly capable of handling my business and you know it. So please, go back to your day off and do whatever it was that you planned to do before your son pulled a fast one."

"I knew exactly what he was up to." His gaze bored into hers with an intensity that sent shivers coursing through her.

"Why are you leading him on?" She plopped a hand to her hip, pinching her side to remind herself to hold firm. "You," she started, and sucked in a breath as the word broke off on the end. "You cannot encourage this behavior. You know as well as I do that he's trying to push us together. It's been bothering me ever since he invited you to eat with us last week."

"You noticed that, too. I was wondering if that's what's been upsetting you." He took a step closer, bringing him so near she had to tilt her chin up to look at him.

"Y-yes, that was it," she said. He was so close the wonderful woodsy scent of his aftershave enveloped her. She wanted to run for cover but refused to cede ground.

"Is that all?" he asked as his gaze shifted to her lips.

Standing her ground might have been a very foolish decision…but like a moth to flame her gaze fluttered to his lips.

Oh, no, you don't!

She spun away and snapped her goggles down over her eyes and snatched the small gas torch. She fumbled to get the flame started. "Go away, Zane." The words came out surprisingly strong considering.

He took the torch from her and instantly had the flame leaping to life. "Hand me a piece of fruit."

She glared at him, snatched up a pear and dropped it into his gloved hand. "Suit yourself. Now, if you will excuse me, I have more tuna to pick."

His chuckle followed her into the barn, where she retrieved her last four buckets. If he wanted to work, then work he would, she thought as she marched from the barn.

The tuna in his hand was burned to a crisp. "Don't burn all my profit up while you're helping me," she snapped. "Oh, and if you're going to insist on this charade, put on a pair of goggles."

"Whatever you say, boss," he teased as he reached for Max's goggles.

"Good." She bobbed her head. "I'll let you work and will finish up out there."

A slow smile bloomed across his face. "You do that. I'm not going anywhere."

His words caused her heart to stall. "Okay, then," she said, turning her back to him and that smile and trying hard to blot out the way those four little words made her feel.

"And, Rose," he said, drawing her to look over her shoulder at him. "If you need me, just call."

"I won't," she said firmly, and marched out into her cactus patch more than determined that she would not need him.

Not ever again.

What was he doing? Zane wondered again as he watched Rose sashay madly into the pasture and disappear behind a massive stand of cactus. Coming out here had been a bad idea. But he hadn't been able to convince himself not to come.

He looked down at the pathetic piece of blackened mush in his hand. He had absolutely no idea what he was doing with Rose or with torching this tuna. All he knew was that when Max had asked Zane to help Rose, he'd said yes. Part of it was because she'd looked lost in church the previous morning after Max had chosen to sit with him. Despite feeling pleasure that his son wanted to sit beside him, Zane had felt no joy in seeing Rose sitting alone.

Not that she would welcome his sentiment. Oh, no. The woman wasn't happy having him here. And, he thought with a rueful smile, if he ruined all of her fruit she would run him off the property with a stick. So he wouldn't ruin it, he thought. He dropped the charred tuna to the side and picked up another one. The hairlike stickers were coming off this time—and only the stickers. He'd watched Max take care of business the week before and so he'd had a great teacher. And as he aimed the flame, he knew working would be much easier without Rose standing near, distracting him with that cute glare of hers.

An hour later when she returned with three buckets filled up and one only half full he had a pile of perfectly toasted tuna. There was plenty still waiting on him, though, so he didn't slow down.

His jaw itched slightly and he rubbed the back of his glove along it and kept on working.

"You're doing good."

Her compliment was unexpected. "I had a good teacher. I just had to concentrate on what he taught me."

She'd calmed down, it seemed. He was relieved, watching as she emptied one bucket onto the table and rinsed it out at the hydrant before she started refilling it with his crispy masterpieces. He enjoyed the moment of quiet calm between them. Even though it was clear her mind was working overtime. He could see it in the set of her jaw, the tilt of her head—it had been that way when he'd first met her. They'd had to spend a lot of time alone and she sat near the fireplace of the safe house and simply watched the fire burn. And he watched her. He'd tried not to, but she'd just drawn him like no other woman he'd ever been around. Before long he'd come to recognize when her thoughts were on her grandmother. She never said she regretted the choice she'd had to make to leave her behind, but he knew it hurt. He wondered, if time were reversed, would she make the same choice knowing what she did now?

He hadn't known the feeling from personal experience until he'd made the decision to leave her, only then did he finally understand exactly what he'd been asking people to do all those years. Only then did he understand how much it ripped out their hearts to walk away.

"You have a limp."

At her soft words the torch slipped a little and he singed the end of his glove with the flame. "And here I thought I'd gotten rid of it." He wasn't sure whether to be irritated that it was still noticeable if someone looked closely enough. Or whether to be encouraged that Rose had just given away the fact that she had looked that closely at him. He'd admitted he'd come here because he couldn't stop thinking about her. But did he want to open up his past to her?

"Was it something from your work?"

"You should know men don't like to talk about their ailments with ladies."

"Were you hurt badly?"

He cocked his head and frowned. "Take a hint. I'd rather not talk about this. Of all the things we could talk about, this is not it."

"But this is what I want to talk about."

"I could leave."

"Fine with me. I didn't ask you here in the first place."

She stared unblinking at him.

He shook his head and gave in—to a point. "Yes, it was work. And, yes, it was bad."

"And?"

"And it took some work to get over. Those twenty steps up to my apartment along with other morning exercises are whipping the final tail end of it." His face was burning where it had been itching earlier. He wiped it hard with his gloved fingers.

"Oh! What are you doing?" Her eyes flared at the

same time that she grabbed on to his wrist and yanked his fingers from his face.

"I have an itch. I'm scratching it."

"Put that down," she demanded, forcing the tuna to fall out of his hand onto the table. "And shut that torch off! Now."

He did as she said, one-handed, not sure why she was so angry. She tore her goggles off her head and tugged their gloves off as she glared at him.

"What?" he asked, really needing to scratch his face.

"I told you not to touch your face."

True, they'd moved on from his injury, but this was not good. And his face was really itching. Burning.

"Come to the house. Don't touch anything."

He followed her as she stormed into the house.

"Sit," she demanded the moment he entered the kitchen behind her. She had her back to him and was digging through a drawer.

His face was really burning and by now he understood his stupidity. Understood exactly what he'd done. His right jaw was on fire and the culprit was a bunch of tiny cactus stickers.

"Where is it?" Rose growled, slamming one drawer shut and yanking open another. He had no idea what she was looking for, but he was surely hoping she found it and soon.

"Got it!" she exclaimed, spinning around with a roll of silver duct tape held high.

"What is *that* for?"

She pulled a length out, bit it with her teeth to start the tear and then ripped it off. "Believe it or not, this is the best way to get those spines out of your jaw."

He refused to run but this didn't look good.

"Don't look so terrified."

"I do not look terrified," he denied. Turning his jaw away as she came at him with the strip of tape that was well-known for its extra firm contact. His jaw could not take extra firm. It felt raw.

"If you're not terrified, then don't turn away," she said.

He gritted his teeth, his jaw flexed and he forced himself to angle it toward her. This was not going to be pleasant. Might even be worse than a trip to the dentist with the way his jaw was sizzling.

She stepped close. "I promise this will help," she said gently. Her sweet breath feathered across his jaw and soothed his soul. "I believe you," he murmured, perfectly still as she laid the tape across his skin. His gaze roved over her face as her fingers trembled against his jaw. He sought her eyes with his own. Their stormy-night darkness called to him.

He swallowed hard; automatically his hand found her waist and he tugged her a step closer…she closed her eyes for a second, her fingers stilled—she was thinking about kissing him as much as he was thinking about kissing her. He smiled just as she opened her eyes and *ripped* the tape off his jaw!

Chapter Thirteen

"You didn't have to enjoy that so much!" Zane cupped his sticker-free jaw and glared at Rose. He wasn't so sure she hadn't taken skin with the stickers.

"You need to leave," she said, wadding the duct tape into a ball, matching his glare with her own.

Zane rubbed his jaw and stared at her. Yes, he lost his head a bit but this was overreacting in a big way. "Don't you think this cat-and-mouse thing has gone on too long? We have to get everything out on the table so we can stop all this foolishness."

"Cat and mouse! Is that what you think I'm doing? Playing games with you?"

"No." He shoved a hand through his hair. She was making him crazy! He moved toward her but she backed away. "Rose," he said, as they two-stepped until she backed into the counter. "You have become one stubborn woman over the years."

"I became what I needed to become, thank you very much."

Zane couldn't stand seeing her bitter, especially knowing he'd caused it, no matter what she'd kept from him. "I'm sorry I left without explaining myself," he said, taking her by the shoulders. She tensed, but her eyes melted for a moment and his heart stalled. "So much has happened that I regret," he said softly. "I missed you so much after I left." He couldn't stop himself from lifting one hand to stroke her cheek. "For the first time ever, I understood what it was like to leave behind someone you cared for deeply. All those years I'd watched witnesses leave family and friends, but had never experienced it for myself. Leaving you made me suffer like you suffered when you left your grandmother behind." He searched her eyes as he lowered his lips toward hers. He'd dreamed of kissing her again for years.

"Is that supposed to make me feel better?" she growled, shrugging his hand off her shoulder and pushing past him.

Zane closed his eyes and berated his bad timing before turning around. She was standing at the door, holding it wide.

"I want you to leave."

Zane was confused. Maybe he shouldn't have tried to kiss her. But he'd just opened his heart to her. "Rose, I thought—"

"What? That your little emotional confession was supposed to make me *feel* better? That one confession and all was right in the world. Here's a news flash for you. If I had been given the option of going back to my gram, I'd have gone in an instant. So don't tell me you suffered what I suffered. You didn't come back."

He'd made a mess of things. "Rose, it wasn't that easy—"

"Oh, really. You want me to tell you a little bit about something not being easy? Because I can do that, Zane. Finding out I was pregnant and you were nowhere to be found… Forgive me if I don't cry for you." She was trembling and the sight tore him up.

"I'm going to go and let you calm down." He paused beside her.

She crossed her arms and set her lips firmly together.

He should go. He knew it but, looking into her eyes, he couldn't do it. Not this time. "I felt like I'd taken advantage of you. I knew you were sad, lonely, and in desperate need of a friend… I was supposed to be your protector. I wasn't supposed to use your situation to my advantage." Surely she could see his side of this.

"And is that what you did? Is that what I was to you, just an easy target?"

"Never." How could he make her understand? "I had never crossed from professional distance into the realm of…having a personal relationship. Of falling for someone."

She dropped her gaze to the floor. But not before he saw her pain.

"I took advantage of you. No excuse." He'd told himself that maybe she didn't see it that way, but he knew she must. It stung while at the same time he knew it was the truth. "That's why I didn't come back for you. I came to Mule Hollow to ask you to forgive me. For everything."

Rose pulled out of his grasp and stalked onto the porch. He went after her. She was in the yard before she finally spun to face him again.

"For years I've taught Max that he's responsible for his actions," she said in a softly controlled voice. "The Bible is very plain about that. Wouldn't you agree?"

"Yes, but—"

"I was a consenting adult, Zane. I was responsible for all of my actions. Yes, I was vulnerable. But I knew what I was doing when I stepped out onto that patio after you'd told me not to. And I also knew what I was doing when I let our relationship get personal. I made that choice. Yes, it was wrong. Obviously, I believed there was more to our relationship than was actually there…but don't belittle me."

Zane was confused. "Belittle you?"

"Yes. Those were my choices. Right or wrong I made them. Don't stand there and say my every move was orchestrated by you. It insults me."

"What?"

Her eyes flashed. "You are standing there in my front yard telling me that I was so stupid that I could be suckered and that's why you ran away and didn't come back! Just leave."

"That isn't what I said. How did you get that out of what I said?"

"Leave. Don't come back." She stomped to his truck and yanked open the door. "Here, I'll show you the way."

Totally and completely baffled, he couldn't move. She, on the other hand, stormed past him, up the steps of her house and slammed the door behind her.

He'd almost kissed her—but worse, she'd almost let him.

Rose didn't stop until she reached her bedroom and had slammed that door, too…she needed as much space between her and Zane as she could get.

Oh, goodness, but she had almost crumbled when he'd wrapped his arms around her and drew her close. How was she going to manage this?

Her heart was still thundering and her legs wouldn't carry her weight any longer. She sank to the stool in front of her dressing table, staring at her reflection in the mirror. Her cheeks were hot pink. She sucked in a halting breath and blinked back the tears threatening to pour out of her eyes. Mad tears. Sad tears. Tears of frustration.

She'd gone out into the cactus field when he'd first arrived, determined not to need help. And now look at her. She'd picked a fight with him so she wouldn't kiss him!

Of course there was consolation in the fact that picking the fight was truly over an issue that was real.

He had told her in so many words that he hadn't come back for her because he felt she was too incompetent to know her own mind. How humiliating was that?

He'd thought she was of a mature, sound mind when she'd chosen to testify and give up her life to go into the WITSEC program. But when it came to being mature enough to comprehend that she'd fallen in love with him—according to him she wasn't capable of that.

She sniffed and grabbed a tissue. Yes, she was vulnerable. Yes, there were extenuating circumstances that influenced the choices she'd made. But she had loved him. And how dare that man tell her what she'd felt hadn't been real.

How dare he tell her that because of that he hadn't come back!

All this time she'd felt a guilt deep down inside for keeping Max hidden from him. It was true. She could admit it now…because today Zane had liberated her from that guilt. It was his own fault that he hadn't known about Max. Zane was the one who'd walked away.

And she was really angry about it. *Dear Lord,* she prayed. *Please help me cope with this anger...and please turn my thoughts from how wonderful his embrace felt!*

Rose truly believed that God had a plan for her life. That He had been with her through everything and that in her trials He was teaching her something. She'd become more reliant on Him during her strange life and she'd learned to be strong and have a great compassion for women in similar circumstances. But she could not understand what she could gain from this torture.

And it honestly made her angry at Zane and at God.

"I think everything is in order," Brady said the following day, closing his desk drawer and pushing out of his chair. "I'll be at the hospital if you need me. But unless it's something I absolutely have to be involved in, I'm leaving everything in your hands."

Zane gave his boss a reassuring nod. "You can count on me. Now go take care of your wife."

The doctors had admitted Dottie into the hospital the day before. Her blood pressure had risen so high they were worried about her and the baby. The last thing Brady needed on his mind was work. Brady shook his hand in a firm grip.

"Thanks. Dottie was right. Your coming here for the job was a godsend."

Zane opened the door for him. "Go. Tell Dottie I'm praying for her. Everyone is."

They walked out onto the sidewalk just as a small crowd came around the corner from Main Street.

"Looks like everyone's heard the news," Zane said.

Brady nodded. "They're good people."

"Hold up," Norma Sue called. "No pun intended," she said, barreling to a halt. The usual suspects flanked her. Esther Mae, Adela. Behind them, Applegate and Stanley. Sam and Pete, who'd obviously closed up shops for a few minutes. Behind them was Lacy and Sheri from the hair salon along with the gals from the real estate office, and also the candy store. And bringing up the end was Rose and Ashby.

"Did y'all just close down the town?" Brady asked, clearly touched by the show of support.

"'Course we did," Sam said. He stepped up and handed Brady an envelope. "That thar's a little collection we took up to help with your expenses while you're a hangin' around the hospital."

Brady stared at the envelope. "I don't know what to say," he said at last. "Y'all didn't have to do this."

"We know." Lacy stepped up and gave him a hug. "We just want you and Dottie to know we love you and will be praying for you all."

Applegate gave a quick grin. "If you don't want to use it fer lunch money then buy that little woman some flours."

"Flo*wers*," Sam amended, causing everyone to chuckle.

App scowled. "Cain't you hear? That's what I said. Buy her some purdy flours."

Zane caught Rose's eye as she bit her lip and her eyes crinkled with laughter. He was still completely confused by their quarrel the day before. He'd realized that he didn't really know Rose. He'd thought he'd known her, but these couple of weeks in Mule Hollow were showing him that the girl he'd protected had become a woman, a mother. She caught him watching her and her expression went cool and remote. She cut her gaze away from him.

Brady cleared his throat and looked touched. "Thank y'all for coming down here and for this. I think that's a great idea, App. Dottie is going to feel real special."

Zane found himself wondering if anyone had ever given Rose flowers. If anyone had ever really made Rose feel special? He moved to the side as everyone gave Brady a hug and then they bowed their heads as Sam said a prayer for God to keep Dottie and the baby safe.

Rose stood with her head bowed and Zane found himself watching her. All types of questions started forming in his head about her. How had her pregnancy gone? Did she have anyone there who cared for her? Who prayed over her? Did David mistreat her while she was carrying Max? How had she felt when she realized she was pregnant and the father of her baby had skipped out on her? His stomach lurched and he loathed himself more in that moment than he ever imagined possible. He knew exactly how she'd felt, because she'd panicked and married a lowlife. *Dear God,* he prayed, blinking back the heat of tears. He had botched up her life. She may have made her own choices, as she'd pointed out so strongly to him. But no man with any integrity would let her take full responsibility. No, he shared in what had happened in her life. He should have been there for her. If he had been there for her, then he would have been there for their son.

He had to find a way to fix this.

Dear God, he began again, *give me guidance here. Help me make this all up to her.*

Sam ended his prayer. "Coffee's on the house," he said as soon as Brady drove off.

"How about iced tea?" Esther Mae asked.

"That, too." Sam took Adela's hand and placed it in the crook of his arm as they started back down the street.

Zane couldn't move.

"Zane," Norma Sue hollered back at him. "Come on. It's coffee time."

"We'll make sure Rose saves a seat for you," Esther Mae called.

"Not if he was the last man on earth," Rose said, drawing startled looks from everyone but Zane. "You sit with him, Esther Mae. I have to get back to work."

Zane watched her disappear around the corner as everyone turned to stare at him.

Chapter Fourteen

On Saturday morning Rose padded into the kitchen and found Max already up. His hair was sticking out all over the place and he looked as if he could have used another couple of hours' sleep.

It crossed her mind that before long she'd wake every morning to a still, quiet house. He'd finish school and move on with his life, leaving her to get on with her own. Alone. She could handle that. She could. Alone was better than being in a bad situation.

"Mornin', Mom, I loaded the jelly in the car for you," he said, pouring a cup of coffee and handing it to her. "You're all ready to roll."

She laughed watching him grab the milk from the icebox. "Aren't you a slave driver."

"Hey, you gotta get out there and sell our product. I'm just doin' my job." He poured himself a glass of milk and set it on the table beside an open jar of jelly and two pieces of toast waiting on his plate.

"What are you going to do this morning?"

Max slathered jelly on his toast. "I'm hanging out with Dad before I go help with the theater. He's gonna park cars again." His eyes sparked playfully. "You want me to tell him you said hello?"

"No. I certainly do not."

"I'm going to. You know you want me to."

"Max Vincent. You will do no such thing. And I mean it."

He set his toast down. "Are you mad at him?"

She almost said no but that would have been a lie. "Yes. Max, you're old enough to understand…your dad and I both love you. But nothing will ever be between us."

"Mom. Give him a chance, will you?"

"Max, stop. We've discussed this." Frustrated beyond words, she carried her cup to the sink. How was she supposed to deal with this…this situation between her and Zane where Max was concerned? Did she just come out and tell Max how angry she was with Zane? "I need to go get dressed. I have a long day ahead of me."

She hated seeing the frown on Max's face as she left the room. But it couldn't be helped. He had to learn there were some boundaries that even he couldn't cross. That it made her heartsick didn't matter. She was the parent and he was the child. And she had more to think about today, as she delivered orders and tried to drum up more business, than how much her son wanted her to fall in love with his dad.

"Mom," he said, coming out of the house later, just before she pulled out of the driveway. "Are you still going to see Dottie tomorrow after church?"

"Yes, a bunch of us are going in Lacy's car. Do you want to go?" Max loved Lacy's 1958 pink convertible. It was a local fixture and all the kids begged her to give them rides.

"No. I was just, um, thinking it'd be good for you to get away with the girls. You know, girl time might help you relax."

She had a sinking feeling that he thought girl time would fix the trouble between her and Zane.

Pulling out of the driveway, she watched Max shrinking in her rearview mirror as he watched her leave. She had a two-hundred-mile round-trip ahead of her and all she was going to think about was what was going on inside Max's head. Because she had the uneasy feeling that the wheels of his mind were turning in hyperdrive.

It was going to be a very long day.

"I'm trying to help them, Norma Sue," Max said. He'd ridden his bike to the theater early so he'd have time to talk to the matchmakers. He glanced around to make sure no one was around the concession stand to overhear what he was talking about. He didn't want word getting back to his mom. That would ruin everything.

Norma Sue frowned. "I don't know, Max. It's one thing for us to do something and it's one thing for you to do something. But for us to *help* you do this… She might think we were teaching you the art of deception."

"But, Norma—"

Norma Sue help up her hand. "No, son. Truth is I know for certain your mom wouldn't appreciate us encouraging you in this. I'm sorry."

Max couldn't believe what he was hearing. "But I thought y'all said you'd help me."

Esther Mae turned pink, but didn't say anything.

"Max," Adela said, "Norma is right. We can't help this time."

He stared from one to the other. "Look, I just need you to help me make them a romantic dinner." They had to agree to help, or he was doomed. He didn't know the first thing about cooking *or* romance. But his pleading didn't faze them—they just looked at each other and then the floor.

"We can't," Adela said, looking at him with gentle eyes. "Max, we *cannot* help you. Our hands are tied."

He couldn't believe it. They'd helped everyone, but not him. It didn't make sense. "Thanks for nothin'," he said, and turned to go. He'd only taken a couple of steps when it hit him. *Our hands are tied.* That's what Adela had said. He twisted around and found them all teary-eyed. "My mom *told* you not to help me. That's it, isn't it?"

Esther Mae nodded, but Norma Sue rammed her with an elbow and she stopped.

"Why?" he asked.

Norma Sue heaved a big sigh. "Look, son, you're old enough to understand this. Your mom is afraid you'll get hurt. She's trying to protect you. The truth is we love you and because of that, we can't be responsible. And we gave our word to your mom."

The sun had just disappeared over the horizon as the caddy made it back to Mule Hollow. Lacy dropped everyone else off first and then headed toward Rose's place. It had been a fun day—after everyone stopped teasing her about Zane—not only about her remark in front of everyone on Friday, but also because she'd avoided him at church. Everyone thought that was quite funny for some strange reason. They had no clue all the turmoil she was feeling.

It felt good seeing Dottie and finding out that she

was doing well. The doctors had decided that they were going to remove the baby by Cesarean on Thursday. It was two weeks earlier than planned, but they'd determined for safety this would be best. Everyone was excited, but the nurses were ecstatic because Brady was driving them nutty!

It was darling, really, with his constant stalking the halls and worrying with her every twinge. The nurses, however, no longer found anything about him cute. Dottie had lovingly informed him she was sending him back to work as soon as they came home from the hospital. Though she'd tried to get him to leave her for a few hours during the day, he'd refused to go any farther than the hotel next door for a shower and a few hours of sleep each night.

Rose was touched by the picture they made and in comparison to her own pregnancy it was like night and day. Oh, to be loved like that. It was an amazing love.

"You sure have been quiet on the ride home," Lacy said as she drove toward Rose's place. "I've been told I'm a good listener if you need to talk." She flashed a sincere smile.

"I was just thinking about Dottie and Brady. They were just so loving toward each other. He is so devoted to her. I'm sure Clint will be the same way with you. It's beautiful."

"You can have it, too. So stop sounding like you've given up. I think if you were willing you would see that you already have someone who loves you. He's just waiting for you to give him the time of day."

Rose sighed and watched the dark shapes of trees and cattle as the car passed them by. "I don't think so."

"Yes, he is. And Max sure would love to have the two of you married."

"I don't know what I'm going to do with him. Most kids would have grown bitter and angry about all of this, but instead he's just taken it in stride. It worries me in some ways and makes me proud of him in others. I mean, what if, deep down, he's more disturbed by all of this than he's letting on?"

"Well, there is no secret that he wants the two of you together. But maybe his easy acceptance comes with y'all moving so much. He just tends to be adaptable or maybe he just knows a good thing when he sees it. Maybe he sees the same thing I see in Zane's eyes when he looks at you. You're in denial is all and he's in love. That's what it is. And a smart kid like Max hasn't missed it."

"I don't know where y'all are all getting that Zane loves me. The man is just now showing up in my life after fourteen years! And besides, I don't love him—"

"You loved him once. Love doesn't die."

"Lacy, that's just wrong. It does die. And besides, it doesn't really matter."

Lacy brought the car to a jolting halt in the center of the road. "You seemed like such a truthful person when we first met." Her lips were twitching at the edges.

"I'm telling the *truth!*"

"Rose, you know a lot of people care about you."

Rose might not have been clear on exactly why they were stopped in the middle of the road, but she knew she had friends in Mule Hollow who cared for her. "Yes, I know. But if you're worried about me, you don't have to be."

Lacy did a rat-a-tat-tat on the steering wheel with her nails. "I'm not worried. I'm…hopeful. That's what I am. I'm hopeful for you finding love. And I'm hopeful that whatever happens in the next little while that you'll keep an open mind. Do you promise me you will?"

Rose's internal antenna went up and she stared at Lacy with now wary eyes. "What does that mean?"

"Nope. I'm serious, Rose, promise me. It's for your own good…and maybe the lives of a few others," she mumbled, which caused Rose more concern, especially as Lacy pinned her with serious, blue eyes. "Promise me you will keep an open mind."

Lacy had done a lot for Rose and the shelter and there was no way Rose could refuse her something she seemed so agitated about. "Certainly I will. For you."

Lacy shook her head. "No. For *you*. Promise you'll keep an open mind for you. And for Max's sake."

Okay, this was odd. But then, Lacy did have her quirks. She was spontaneous, compulsive and completely undeniable. "I promise. Now, what is this all about?"

Lacy answered by stomping the gas! The car shot forward like a pink rocket, slamming Rose back into the seat as if they'd just made liftoff.

"Sorry," Lacy hollered over the wind as her pale blond hair danced about her face. "But we're late."

Rose suddenly had a bad feeling…and it was more than the uncomfortable feeling of her lunch being forced back up her esophagus!

And then, around the bend in the road, she saw Zane's truck at the entrance of her driveway.

Lacy slammed to a tire-screeching stop. "This is as far as I go."

"What? Wait."

Lacy placed a hand on her arm. "I can't wait and I can't explain. I can tell you that I'm fulfilling a favor to that wonderful kid of yours. He specifically instructed me to make you ride up to the house with Zane. How he got Zane here for your arrival I don't have a clue."

"Nothing is wrong with Max, is there?"

"No. He's fine. If you don't hurt him, he should make it through the night in one piece." She happily pointed for her to look at Zane as he walked around the front of his truck. He looked ten feet tall in the beam of the headlights. When he opened her door, she could only look up at him in confusion.

"May I?" he asked, holding his hand out to her.

Rose glanced back to Lacy and found no support when she lifted a brow and smiled. "Go. Don't be mad and please remember they're all crazy about you. So don't kill them."

"Them?" Rose asked. "The matchmakers?"

"Now hold on. Stop jumping to conclusions," Lacy demanded. "Oh, and hey, there, Zane. Same goes for you. No arresting known culprits and throwing away the keys over the next few hours." She blinked up at him then gently shoved Rose. "Now go. Your son has been *very* busy."

Zane chuckled. "No jail time will be involved with tonight."

Rose studied Zane's outstretched hand and met his gaze. She couldn't put a name on the emotion coiling around her chest.

Lacy gave her another nudge. "Go on, honey. Don't ruin this for Max."

"For Max," Rose said, finally finding her voice.

Zane gave up waiting for her to take his hand and took her by the shoulders and pulled her out of the car. "C'mon. Let's go. Max called and I came out only to be told to wait here for you. And that when you got here, I was to bring you to the barn."

Rose entire face crinkled in consternation. "What is he up to?"

Seemingly at ease with the entire situation, Zane lifted one broad shoulder. "Beats me. But I'm game to find out. How about you?"

Behind them Lacy laughed. "Y'all have fun!" she called and swung the giant car around in the road. Rose watched in dismay as she lifted an arm in the air and waved while roaring off…leaving Rose stranded in her own driveway with the last man on earth she wanted to be stranded with—and worse, absolutely no idea what waited for her up the lane!

Chapter Fifteen

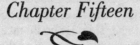

Zane didn't let Rose's cold stare hurt his ego. She was apprehensive, after all. So was he for that matter. But his curiosity about what Max had cooked up had taken the upper hand and was driving him to see what was going on.

"Surely you aren't scared to go see what Max and the ladies have cooked up?"

"Of course I'm not afraid—"

"Then prove it by moving those cute feet of yours. Let's go. He's waiting up at the barn."

She frowned.

"Smile, Rose. This is an adventure," Zane said, opening the door for her. As soon as she was inside, he jogged around to his side and slammed the door behind him. Anticipation filled him. What was Max up to? Something told him it was going to be good.

He just hoped Rose took Lacy's sound advice and let Max have his fun.

The barn doors were closed as they drove up. The kitchen door was open and the only light was the rectangle that stretched from the lighted doorway across the yard. Zane could feel eyes on him. He knew when he was being watched, the hair on the back of his neck had always stood up…except once, with Rose. He pushed the memory away, focused on now.

There was no danger tonight. "Wait," he said, when Rose started to open her door. "Don't move." She looked at him like she was going to string him up. He tried not to look too pleased about what was going down, but it was hard as he closed his door firmly and strode around to her side. He could take a wild guess that Max was giving him points for acting the gentleman. Zane found he liked the idea himself.

"Relax," he said, taking her elbow. "We're being watched." He leaned close to her ear, breathing in the scent of fresh air and vanilla. "Hate me tomorrow, but let's let Max have this night. Please."

She turned and their noses bumped. Zane smiled and resisted the need to kiss her—his inability to resist her had ruined one afternoon already. "Please," he repeated instead.

"Okay. But when his heart gets crushed, it's your fault."

Zane stared into Rose's serious eyes and knew, no matter what had happened before no longer mattered to him. "I have no intention of letting Max's heart get crushed." He would win Rose's heart. Looking at her, he knew he'd never wanted anything in his life as much as this. Suddenly everything was clear and for the first time in his life, he was fighting for his own future and that of the ones he loved. This was one battle he had no intention of losing.

The door to the barn slowly creaked open and Max walked out. The kid was in his Sunday best, black slacks and a white shirt and tie. He had a cloth napkin folded over one arm like a maître d'. Zane's curiosity was piqued more.

"Hello," Max said, his tone formal. "Welcome." He bowed and swept his arm out wide. "Please follow me."

Rose met Zane's curious gaze as they followed Max into the barn…and there they froze.

Zane couldn't believe it—the kid had really been busy!

"It's beautiful," Rose gasped. There were Christmas tree lights strung from every available roost. They glittered in various color combinations and brought tears to her eyes. In the center of the barn was an elegantly set table with a white cloth and candles.

Shock gave way to an unexpected thrill that stole over Rose. She looked up at Zane and her insides curled into a warm ball at his expression. He was in awe, too, and seeing the delight on his usually stern face unraveled her defenses a little.

"What do you think?" Max asked, grinning impishly.

"It's lovely."

"I knew you'd like it!" He crossed to the table and pulled out a chair. Bending at the waist, he reentered his character once more.

Rose's heart squeezed tight and she wanted to cry. How could she tell him this wasn't going to work?

"After you," Zane said, looking as impish as his son. His hand on her arm, he guided her to her chair. The electrical current of his touch vaporized her welling tears. Her heart began pounding like an electric drum.

No sooner had he sat down across from her than Max grabbed a pitcher of tea from a table against the wall and carefully poured tea into their glasses. A romantic, Italian ballad played in the background.

"Y'all visit," Max said. "I'll be back with your food, but it won't be too soon."

Zane chuckled as soon as Max disappeared, and Rose kicked him under the table.

"Kicking me isn't going to stop me from enjoying this."

"Well, don't enjoy it too much," she warned, as much for him as for herself. She had to keep her common sense through this. Nothing had changed between them. But that didn't stop her heart from thudding as Zane laid his hand on top of hers.

"I always enjoy being around you."

She took a deep breath denying that his words didn't mean something to her. Her gaze dropped to their hands, but her throat wouldn't work.

"And I also care about every aspect of your life," he added, rubbing his thumb across her knuckles. "I know you are upset with me. But I wish you would give me—us—a chance. You have to know by now that I'm sorry for leaving."

Every nerve in her body came alive at his gentle touch. Every emotion in her heart reacted to his plea.

She tugged her hand from beneath his and placed it in her lap. "Zane—" She felt trapped.

"Wait," he said, cutting off her protest with a knowing smile. "Before you tell me that's a crazy idea, let's back up and talk about something else. How did your road trip go Saturday?"

He was purposely changing the subject, and Rose was actually thankful to take the conversation to a safe topic. "Not as good as I'd hoped, but it's still a start."

He placed his elbows on the table and cupped his hands. "When do you go to the bank?"

What? How did he know—

"Don't look so startled. Remember, Max told me that you were trying to get a loan so you could expand."

Max. "Next Monday," she said, having forgotten that exchange. She wondered what else about her personal business Max had been telling him.

"Do you think you'll get the business loan?"

She pulled her napkin off her plate and smoothed it across her lap. So maybe this wasn't such a safe topic after all. It was very personal to discuss her financial situation. But then, again, what did she have to hide? "I'm not sure. I think the plan is solid and I'm not really asking for that much. But I don't have a very long credit history. And it does have a few blank spots, as you know."

He grimaced, knowing she was referring to the program. "I could make some calls."

"*No.* I don't want the Justice Department involved in my life anymore," she said and meant it.

"Okay. Don't get agitated. I don't understand your reasoning, but I'll respect it. Can I ask how you bought this place?"

"The owners financed it for me on the recommendation of my friends here in town. The town's done so much for everyone who came here from the shelter."

"What if a friend wanted to finance your business?"

"If you're saying you would do that then the answer is a firm no."

"Why not? I believe in the idea. I believe in you and Max. And I have a personal interest in it."

This topic had quickly gone south. "Just because Max is your son doesn't mean—"

Zane reached across the table and laid his hand over hers again. She was going to have to remember to keep her hands off the table!

"Max is an interest…but I was talking about you."

"Zane—"

The door creaked open and Rose yanked her hand from Zane's. She bit her upper lip as Max entered, carrying a large tray. He set the tray on the table where he'd placed the tea pitcher earlier. When he turned to them, he was carrying a basket of bread. He grinned as he placed it on the table.

Though they were being served Italian food, Rose was very aware that there was no garlic on the bread. That little *scoundrel!*

Still, though she was upset, she couldn't say anything. Instead she watched him retrieve plates of steaming spaghetti from the tray and set them in front of her and Zane.

"Sam made this, so y'all know it's going to be delicious."

"Sam," she said, startled.

"Yeah, good ol' Sam to the rescue," he said, and winked at her. "Now, this night is for y'all. Eat, drink and have a good time. Talk. Relax. I'll bring dessert later. But take your time. Enjoy."

Enjoy! She felt like she was in a squeeze chute looking from Max to Zane!

She had to put a stop to this before it got any further out of control. She started to stand, but Zane's hand on her arm stopped her.

"Thank you, son," he said, gently pressing her arm. She relaxed into her seat, holding his gaze.

"Okay, then," Max said, drawing her to look up at him. He wore the bright, expectant look of a puppy as he took one more look at his handiwork before heading out the door, wearing his heart on his sleeve.

Oh, Max.

Rose didn't know whether to laugh or cry watching him disappear. When he firmly closed the barn door she glared at Zane, feeling trapped.

"Bread?" Zane asked, cocking a brow and holding the basket up. "I'm planning to do as he says and enjoy this moment. How about you? Are you game to push everything aside for the evening and just be two people on a date?" His eyes twinkled like amber honey in sunlight…or candlelight to be more dangerously exact.

The food smelled fabulous. The soft music *was* romantic. And Zane Cantrell by candlelight was quite honestly irresistible. Rose took a shuddering breath… What to do?

With a sigh, she did the only thing she could do under the circumstances.

She nodded.

"But this is just for tonight. Don't get any ideas," she said, pulling her head out of the clouds and planting her feet firmly on solid ground. Irresistible or not, Zane was not getting under her skin.

"Scout's honor. I won't get any ideas."

The man thought he was so cute—that he was cute was irrelevant. Everyone was getting what they wanted tonight while she was being forced into an impossible situation. "I mean it, Zane. We are pretending to be two normal people on a *normal* date. That's all. But for the record, I don't believe this is good for Max. It's only giving him mixed signals. And it's promoting behavior that I'm not all that thrilled with. I've already told him that he needs to forget this idea that you and I are going to get together."

Zane's jaw tightened. "Are you going to start pretending any time soon? Because I'm not feeling it yet."

She'd aggravated him. Well, it couldn't be helped. "Fine," she grunted and took an exaggerated breath, expelling it slowly. "Okay. Let the show begin."

His lips flattened momentarily and he looked like Max when he was contemplating something seriously. "Are you sure?"

She nodded. She decided that she could use the time to assuage her relentless curiosity about the years between the last time she'd seen him and his reappearance. There were burning questions that begged to be answered. And since this truce was his idea, he could pay for it with information.

"So," she began, taking a piece of bread from the basket he'd been patiently holding out to her. Her taking the bread was the ultimate symbol of a truce. He looked pleased with himself when she took a slice. He did the same.

"So," he echoed.

Her insides fluttered like new wings on a butterfly, acknowledging things she didn't want to acknowledge. What if this was truly a beginning? What if she really let her defenses down and believed happy endings happen to women like her?

Surely she wasn't the first woman who felt compelled to cling to her independence because she needed the security and peace of mind derived from it. She was carving out her own happy ending. Just not one with the white knight sweeping her off her feet.

She'd given up on that the morning she walked into the safe house kitchen and Zane was gone…and then she'd learned with David that if she kept expecting a man to give her a happy ending then she might be condemned to a life of pain and disappointment.

Nope, she was just fine with creating her own happy ending and she reminded herself of this as she ate. If she depended on only herself, she could survive just fine. And just fine was much better than heartache.

"You loved being a Texas Ranger. Are you going back to it?" she asked, shifting the focus to him.

He smiled. "No. I live here now."

"But you loved it. You were good at it. The best."

The light that had been dancing in his eyes dimmed. "We both know I wasn't."

The wave of protectiveness that surged over her startled her. His ability to protect her had never been an issue. It was unbelievable that he would think such a thing. "You were the best. What happened with me was my fault. You told me to stay inside. You did everything in your power to protect me, but I went outside anyway. Foolishly ignored your warnings."

"I should have made you understand the probability that at that crucial time before the trial, danger was imminent."

"There was an internal leak, Zane. Otherwise I most likely would have been safe."

"That's no excuse. There is always the probability of a breakdown. And I came after you and was so caught up in my need to kiss you that I didn't see the attack coming. That's the problem." He slammed his hand on the table.

So much for a romantic meal! "You didn't see it because I was throwing myself at you. And if you hadn't taken me in your arms at that very instant, I very well could be dead!" This was crazy—what was she doing?

He shook his head. "You're alive because God kept you alive. Not because of what I did."

"Oh, please. You were the one who threw me to the ground and covered me with your body. You're the one who got me behind that table and then used yourself as a shield to get me inside. God saved me that day by using you. I can't believe you don't realize that."

His jaw tensed but he didn't say anything. The song in the background ended and the silence between the next one to play seemed to echo around them as they squared off across a vivid line of battle. "You know what?" he said. "You'll never change my view of that, Rose. But my concern now is for the future." He picked up his fork. "We better eat some of this now before Max gets his feelings hurt."

Rose watched him take a big bite of his spaghetti and then smile as if they weren't fighting. The man was really infuriating—but charming! She picked up her fork, twirled it in the noodles and tried not to think too much. She was drowning in very confusing waters.

"I bought that house I was looking at," he said finally, then took a big drink of his tea. His Adam's apple bobbed with each swallow. "I'd like it if you'd come out and take a look at the place."

Rose's mouth went dry. His gaze was unnerving. "I'm not sure that's a good idea."

"It's a very good idea. After all, Max will be spending a lot of time there. And it only makes sense that you should check the place out, don't you think?"

Rose's breath caught. She'd put the idea out of her mind that Zane might still be thinking of getting custody of Max. Now the possibility was back on the table.

"Right," she said tightly. "Now that you point that out, I would like to see it."

He gave her a knowing smile. "That's what I thought. I'm moving in tomorrow. How about coming by?"

"Sure," she said. What else could she say? "But I can't tomorrow. You know what? You have avoided answering my question over and over. Are you planning to try to get custody of Max? It's time for you to tell me what your intentions are. You were the one who said we were playing cat-and-mouse games."

"What happened to us having a nice romantic dinner?"

"That's just it. How in the world do you and everyone else in this town expect me to not think about this?" The more she thought about it the madder she got. "Nothing about this is working for me." She pushed back from the table and was fully intent on walking out. "I'm calling this charade off."

Zane grabbed her arm. "Wait. Please don't go."

She glared at him, but said nothing, clearly waiting for an answer.

"The answer is no," he said at last. "I'm not going to sue for custody of Max. So relax. He's old enough to make up his own mind about things anyway. Putting him in a position to have to choose is not something I would ever do to him. And we both know he would choose you."

Rose swallowed hard at what she saw in his eyes and heard in his voice. So much regret. So much love. Tears filled her eyes and she had to look away. This was so hard. The entire situation.

The barn door opened and Max entered. Zane leaned close to her. "Please don't cry. Can you relax now so we can get back to being nice to each other? I personally like us better that way."

Rose nodded, and before Max reached them she dabbed at her damp eyes.

She hated feeling vulnerable. She hated it more than anyone could ever know. Looking at Zane and then at Max looking as sweet as the plates of chocolate cake he carried, she felt depleted emotionally. She should have been happy hearing Zane wasn't going to cause her child to have to meet the judicial system unnecessarily. But even that news couldn't change the fact that Max was rooting for a happy ending to this story…and Rose knew she couldn't give it to him.

Chapter Sixteen

"So, did you have a good time?" Max asked the next morning. He'd already asked her several times before he went to bed the night before. The kid had been thrilled with himself and she'd not been able to burst his bubble of pleasure.

She'd smiled through the rest of the evening and then gone to bed completely traumatized by the entire evening. Over and over she'd found herself praying for some kind of peace about the situation. But none came.

God didn't work so suddenly for the most part—sometimes He did—yet she knew through experience that most of the time problems worked out slowly. Looking at Max now, she knew she couldn't wait. Max needed to know the truth. Drawing this out was only going to hurt him more.

"Max, I need to be straight with you. I had a good time. But you need to understand that nothing is going to happen between your dad and me. The last thing I want is to hurt you. But, babe, you've got to promise me you won't do any more matchmaking."

"Mom, why won't you give Dad a *chance?*" He rammed his chair back and stood.

Rose wasn't prepared for the out-and-out belligerence in Max's tone. Or the uncharacteristic anger.

She stood at the sink. "Max, he's here in town where you can see him as much as you want. You must know that he wants you in his life? That's what matters."

"He wants us in his life. Mom, can't you see that? He loves you. But you are so *stubborn.*"

"Max! I don't love Zane."

"I don't believe you. And I always believe you. It's like you're scared of this with Dad." She flinched at his tone and he stopped suddenly and stared at her. "That's it, isn't it?"

Rose fidgeted with the cup towel, feeling as if she were under a microscope. Yes, she was afraid, but it was more.

"Mom, you've never been afraid of anything. How can you be afraid of Dad?"

She sat down in the chair across from him, owing him an explanation.

"Max. This is about more than just Zane." How did she put this? There were so many reasons for her to feel at peace with her decisions. "It's more like I just don't feel like this is what God has for me. When I'm around him I'm in constant turmoil. I don't have any peace about giving up my independence. I've had to fight so hard to have it. I'm settled. I'm happy. It's not that I'm actually afraid of Zane, but rather of messing up. Again."

"Mom, you're like supermom. You're my hero. But you gotta believe what you're always preaching to me. You know, that it's okay to mess up, because at least if you're messing up, you're learning." He was giving her a pep talk.

"That's different. In this situation I wouldn't be learning anything. Except that I'd messed up. And I don't want or need that. I have everything I want right here."

Max shook his head and left the table. He didn't look mad any longer, but the disappointment in his eyes bothered her worse.

"What's on your agenda for today?" she called, feeling horrible as he walked away. Monday was normally her day off but Ashby had asked her to work today because she had to go out of town for something. She hadn't thought much about it then, but now watching Max she wished she didn't have to leave him alone.

He looked so forlorn, trudging down the hall with his shoulders slumped. "I'll probably just watch TV," he said and slammed his bedroom door. Closed it between them like a blow from his heart to hers.

And it hit its target dead center.

"Heard y'all had quite a time out at Rose's last night," Sam said as soon as Zane walked into the diner. App and Stanley grinned at him as did several cowboys who were eating breakfast.

"Your spaghetti was great." Zane slid onto a stool and lifted a brow at Sam. "You never told me you were a matchmaker, too."

He gave a mischievous grin. "I ain't normally. But Rose told Adela and the girls to back off, so somebody had ta help out the poor kid."

"Did it work?" App called.

Zane rubbed his temple; he had the beginnings of a headache that came from no sleep and a head and a heart doing battle with each other. "I guess only time will tell, Applegate. Sam, I'm going to advise you to hide if you see Rose coming."

Sam chuckled, "Ya think?"

"Yep, but first can you give me a coffee to go? I'm moving into my place today—in between keeping the peace around here." That got him a few chuckles. Zane meant it as a joke but there was part of him that still couldn't get used to the way things were here in Mule Hollow. He felt like he could become complacent here and for a man who'd lived his life constantly on the edge, where a moment of complacency could cost a life…he was having a hard time adjusting. Brady seemed to have done it and yet, he still seemed reliable, capable. Zane was determined to adjust to this new lifestyle. Especially after talking with Rose last night.

He'd gone home with a lot to think about. He'd let go of any remaining anger he'd felt at Rose as they'd talked. Though it was clear she might not ever get past what he'd done to her.

"Here's yor coffee. So you need any help moving in out thar?"

"Thanks, Sam. And no. I'll be basically camping until my things arrive out of storage. What I have with me will fit in the front seat of my truck."

"You gonna git Rose ta decorate fer ya?" Stanley asked, as he reached for a handful of sunflowers.

Zane thanked Sam for the coffee and paid up. "I don't know, Stanley, maybe you need to put in a good word for me. She had dinner with me last night, but I'm not sure it changed her feelings toward me."

"Seriously?" he asked.

"'Fraid so. I think I'm going to need more intervention than even you or the Mule Hollow matchmakers can give me."

App scrubbed his chin. "Maybe you need ta take some positive action of yer own—if you want Rose." He looked toward the table of cowboys. "Or maybe you'd rather wait until one of these lamebrains gets smart and goes and woos her off her feet."

One of the cowboys grinned and started to say something, but Zane shot him a warning glare that had him digging into his pancake instead.

"That's what I thought," App said with a smug grin.

"You fellas have a nice day," Zane said, deciding the conversation had gone as public as he cared for it to go. As he got in his truck and pulled onto Main Street, Rose drove up and parked in front of the dress store. His adrenaline spiked seeing her and for a guy who'd just been thinking he was losing his edge, every fiber of his being went on red alert.

He watched as she got out of her car. Yes, he sat right there in the middle of the street blocking traffic, if there had been any traffic, and watched her. She saw him and instead of turning a cold shoulder she strode toward him.

"Good morning," she said, stopping a couple of feet from his open window. She looked as far from happy as a person could look.

"What's wrong?" he asked, skipping the pleasantries. She was about to tell him that the entire evening had been a mistake and she never wanted to see him again—which would be hard since he wouldn't be able to give her what she wanted.

"It's Max."

Alarm shot through Zane. "Is he okay?"

She nodded but didn't look convincing. "I mean

he's not lost in the woods or anything. But, well…"
She looked tearful and her gaze slid away before
coming back to him. "I think maybe you should go
talk to him. I mean, I don't really know what to do for
him. And maybe…" She swallowed hard and Zane
knew asking for his help had to be hard for her.
"Maybe he needs his dad to explain all of this…you
know, *this*."

"Yeah, I know what this is," Zane said, trying to
give her a little help. "Did something happen?"

She nodded. "He's really angry with me."

"I'll head out there right now."

"Thanks."

Zane watched her go into the shop. Then he headed
toward her house. She had asked for his help with
their son. His heart filled with hope. But he also knew
that something big must have happened between her
and Max. And that worried him.

He found Max in the barn tearing down lights.

"Max, what are you doing?"

"I'm getting rid of these stupid lights."

Zane took a moment to let the angry words sink in
before he moved forward and started unraveling a
strand of lights from the top railing of a stall. "Do you
want to talk about it?"

"About what? There's nothing to talk about."

"If that's the case, then why are you so mad?"

From beneath lowered brows, Zane watched Max's
jaw tense before he jerked down another strand. He
threw the shredded lights on the ground and glared at
Zane. His thin body was rigid, his fists clenched at his
sides.

"All my life she's been a fighter. Telling me…" He

smashed his fist against his side. "Telling me that as long as I kept getting up when things went wrong that *that* was what counted. That it created strong character. That it's not what happens to us but how we react to it that makes us strong."

"I think that's good advice. And true." And it sounded like Rose.

"Oh, yeah, well, it's a lie! Just like half the stuff she ever told me. You, her life in the witness protection program, our life in those shelters—everything. But the biggest lie of all is that she got back up. She didn't get back up."

Zane had questions bounding around in his head but he kept silent. The kid needed to expel these feelings. Rose had said from the beginning that Max was taking things too well. She'd been right and he hadn't taken it seriously enough.

"She never did," Max said again in disgust. "She's not brave like I thought. She's afraid."

"Afraid of what?"

"Of you."

"Of me?" Zane felt blood thundering in his head, pounding away. He knew Rose was afraid but the last thing she'd want was for Max to know it. The kid was too smart for his own good.

"Yeah, she's afraid of messing up. She said so. And messing up means she's afraid if she marries you and you turn out to be a jerk she'll have messed up again."

"She has every right to be afraid."

Max's face fell. "Of you?"

Zane nodded. "Yes."

"But you're a Ranger. You're a deputy. She should know you're not going to hurt her."

"C'mon, Max. You know full well this has nothing

to do with me lifting a hand to harm her. We're talking about her heart here. And a heart isn't always as tough as we want it to be. I have already hurt her heart." Zane prayed for the right words to help Max because he felt helpless looking at him.

"It doesn't bother you knowing she loves you but that she doesn't want to be with you?" Max asked, breathing hard, his chest heaving as if he'd just finished a race.

Zane gave a derisive laugh. "It bothers me more than I can express. But, Max, I'm part of the reason she's like this. I *left* her. It doesn't matter why or that I didn't know about you. It doesn't matter that in my head I thought I was doing right by her. She's not just scared. Max, she's hurting and holding it back just as much as you've been doing ever since you found out she lied to you."

Max spun toward the fence and kicked it so hard Zane feared the board or the foot would break. "Yeah, let out some of that anger. It's okay. You're allowed. And your mom is allowed to be angry, too. She is a remarkable woman. It's just that everything is catching up and she's having to adjust to it just like you are. Just like I am. This can't happen overnight. We might want it to. But it can't."

Swiping his sleeve across his eyes, Max turned back to face Zane. His eyes were bright and rimmed in red. Zane wanted to yank him into his arms and hug him tight; instead, he laid a hand on his shoulder.

"You know. I didn't sleep much last night. Spent it thinking and asking the Lord to show me the way. I looked up a verse in first Corinthians, bits and pieces of it kept ringing through my head and I wanted to read it in its entirety. Do you know the one I'm talking about?"

Max's gaze shifted to his feet. "Corinthians," he said, looking thoughtful. "That's Paul, right?"

Zane nodded. Knowing Rose had raised Max up in church, helping him develop a strong relationship with the Lord meant the world to him.

"Is that the one about love is patient and kind? I see that one written on wall hangings all the time."

Zane smiled. "Yeah, that one. Well, that part of the verse is the most popular and it's true in this instance very much so. If you love your mom, you will be patient and kind right now. But it's the part of the verse toward the end that God spoke to me with. If you want to read the whole passage, it's 1 Corinthians 13:1–7. Verse seven says that love always protects, always trusts, always hopes, always perseveres."

Beneath Zane's hand Max's shoulder heaved up then down as he sucked in a long, deep breath. Zane let his hand drop and waited.

With stronger eyes Max looked up at him. "Is that what you're doing right now?"

Zane nodded. "I don't know what will happen with your mom and me. But God knows…and I'm trusting, hoping and hanging in there, persevering with those things in my heart. But it's the protecting part that God had jump off the page at me. I love you, son. I'll always be here for you to protect and guide you no matter what happens between me and your mom. But right now, I'm trying to protect her heart. It needs time. I know God put this verse on my heart to help me understand."

Max looked around the barn. Zane knew he was looking at all the lights. "I was rushing her with all of this."

"Maybe a little. But it came from your heart and

there is no fault there. It might have been just what we needed to jolt her forward. Who knows? I'd have never thought in a million years to do something like that." He laughed. "And I loved it!"

"You did?"

"Yeah, you might have turned your ol' dad into a romantic."

Max laughed and rolled his eyes. "I think girls like that sappy stuff."

"I think you're going to make some girl very happy one of these days. But for now, how about that cactus patch out at my house you were so anxious for me to buy? What say you put your dreams back on track and come help me move in and then we get to work?"

"Sounds like a plan."

Zane gave in and pulled him in for a hug. "You're doing great, kid." Max hugged him back and Zane had never felt as perfectly at peace and grateful to be alive as he did in that moment.

Chapter Seventeen

On Wednesday morning Rose was dropping an order of jelly at Pete's when Zane walked in. She smiled, feeling grateful, for whatever he'd said to Max on Monday, it had worked. Max seemed more like his old self and was now working at Zane's each day harvesting the patch of prickly pear. She hadn't pushed to find out what had been said, feeling at peace with the idea that maybe she didn't need to know.

Ashby had announced on Tuesday morning that she was expecting a baby and Rose had been thrilled. As was everyone else. But despite Ashby's wonderful news, Rose had still had to endure three days of questions about how her special dinner date had gone. It had been stressful enough trying to convince everyone that nothing had changed. Except, looking at him now, she knew that something had. She didn't feel angry at him anymore.

But that was it. She was accepting that maybe they could live in the same town and share their son.

Looking at him as he strode into the store, she told

herself that the kick to her pulse was simply because she was startled that he was a mess. There was mud caked to his boots and the bottoms of his jeans and even his shirt was damp. It was only nine o'clock!

"What happened to you?" Pete asked the question she wanted to ask.

Zane looked sheepish and Rose smiled as he hung his head momentarily.

"You know that donkey that Cort and Lilly Wells have?"

"Samantha," Pete said. "Everyone knows that donkey."

"And so do I now. I was on my way into town this morning and saw her. She'd gotten herself stuck in the mud in that cow pond up near the road. I had to go get Cort to help me get her out of her little situation. It was a chore and a half."

"I'm so glad you saw her," Rose said. "Is she okay? Lilly would really have a hard time if anything happened to her sweet Samantha."

Zane looked amused. "She's fine. She grinned over her shoulder at me with those big lips the whole time I was trying to push her fat little bottom out of the mud. Cort was on the other end with a rope."

Pete hooted. "Sounds like you got the bad end of that deal. But that donkey grins at everyone. That donkey is a regular prankster."

Rose laughed. "She's funny, all right. Why didn't y'all offer her some banana taffy?"

Zane looked pained. "That's how we got her out finally. Lilly got there after a bit since she'd had to take time to get the baby up. But once she got there with her pocket full of that yellow taffy and waved it under the ol' girl's nose she popped right out of that mud."

He shook his head. "It was the strangest thing I've seen."

"That's Samantha. She was probably just having a little spa time," Pete said, grinning. "Was there something you needed? Besides a bath?"

"No, nothing, Pete. I was actually looking for Rose. Would you mind if I stole her for a moment and have a word with her?"

Pete looked from Zane to Rose. "I don't mind if she don't."

"Sure," Rose said, as she took the last jar of jelly out of the crate and set it on the counter by the other ones. Zane reached for the empty crate at the same time she did and their hands touched. Her pulse quickened like quicksilver and she immediately drew back.

"I can carry that," she said even as he carried it toward the door. "I'm capable," she said, following him.

"I'm sure you are," he said. "But I'm doing it anyway." He grinned over his shoulder at her like they were best friends.

And just like that her temper at him flared—or maybe it was just being near him that made her feel so vulnerable and scared and flustered that she was mad at herself and not him.

She hurried from the feed store and opened her back door, waiting as he set the crate inside. He was a mess and she found herself envisioning him stuck in the mud with Samantha and she couldn't help smiling.

He straightened and caught her. "Hey, stop laughing."

"I'm sorry. It's just, I'm sure you didn't know keeping the peace in Mule Hollow would involve rescuing banana-taffy-loving donkeys."

He turned a tinge of pink. "No, I didn't. It's a whole other world here."

"Yes, it is," she said, holding his gaze for a beat as they seemed to both think back in time.

"Everything better at home?" he asked, at last, filling the awkward moment.

"Yes. I don't know what you said to Max, but he seems more like himself."

"Good. He was just wound up. He'll be okay. He's been working real hard the past couple of days."

She nodded, trying to relax, but the conversation seemed forced, stilted. She was simply too tense standing beside Zane.

"So, when are you going to come out and see the place? I'm basically camping there right now while I wait on my things to arrive from storage. But I'd like to show you the place. And talk."

She was so tempted. She'd been praying that God would ease her mind and her heart where Zane was concerned. It hadn't happened yet. All she felt was stomach-churning turmoil as she looked up at him. "I really can't today. I've got jelly to make after work."

He rammed his hands into his jeans and looked so much like a disappointed Max that she couldn't take it. "Maybe tomorrow evening, though."

He smiled. "Sounds like a plan."

She smiled, both from the smile on his face and that he'd stolen Max's quote.

"Are you going to the hospital in the morning?" he asked.

"Yes, the same group who went Sunday are leaving before daylight. I'm so excited for Dottie and Brady."

"Yeah, they seem pretty excited." He stepped back but looked almost as if he didn't want to leave. "I better get back home and cleaned up so Mule Hollow isn't embarrassed by their law enforcement. Y'all be safe and I'll see you tomorrow."

Rose watched him hop into his truck, then she hurried across the street to the store. Her legs were as wobbly as they'd been the day he'd first come to town. The torture just never seemed to end where the man was concerned.

"Y'all should have seen Zane and Cort!" Lilly Wells said over the wind. They were in the big pink convertible speeding down the highway, with the top down. Rose was sitting in the backseat between Molly, the reporter, and Lilly. Lacy was driving and Sheri was riding shotgun. Lacy and Sheri both had on fluorescent ball caps, but their short wispy hair was still dancing around their ears. Molly also had on a ball cap with her long ponytail sticking out the back but Rose and Lilly hadn't thought about hats. Looking at Lilly with her dark corkscrew tendrils whipping in the wind like string cheese in a mixer, she was afraid of what her own hair was going to look like when she got to the hospital.

"He said you got her out with taffy," Rose said.

Lacy glanced over her shoulder, her eyes wide. "Oh, did he now! Did y'all have a nice conversation about it?"

Rose blushed and looked to the side, only to be met by Molly's inquiring gaze. The last thing she wanted was for Molly to go writing about her and Zane in her newspaper column. "I just spoke to him briefly. That's all. Absolutely no news there," she said to Molly.

"Don't worry," she said. "I'm not writing about you and Zane. Given your background, you know, hiding out and all, I just don't think me plastering y'alls romance across the nation would be a good thing. Even if you are supposed to be out of danger now."

Well, that at least was a blessing. Except she had said romance. "There isn't any romance."

"And just why not?" Lilly asked. "He was so cute yesterday. You should have seen him all big heroic man that he is back there with his shoulder pressed to Samantha's rump. You know, poor thing is the size of a small elephant. And she kept slapping him in the face with her tail." Lilly chuckled. "I told her it wasn't very nice but she just grinned. Truth is, though, I didn't tell the men this but she could have walked out of the mud anytime she wanted."

"So why didn't she?" Rose asked; the picture of Zane and the donkey made her smile.

Lacy hooted from the front seat. "Because Lilly had her on a diet. That's why!"

Lilly nodded. "Bingo! She needs to lose weight desperately but she'll do anything for banana taffy. The sneak. Even pretend to get stuck in the mud. The only reason I gave it to her yesterday was because I didn't want to embarrass poor Zane. I mean the man was really, *reallly* working hard to save her! How could I let him know she was hoodwinking him?"

Rose got tickled. She couldn't help it. Poor Zane. "I think you were right. He probably doesn't need to know the truth."

Their hoots of laughter trailed out behind them as Lacy guided the big car around a curve. Rose felt light-hearted and happy suddenly. And for the rest of the drive her mind stayed dangerously on Zane.

Chapter Eighteen

The hospital waiting room was packed.

Rose, along with half of Mule Hollow, waited for the doctor to come and give them good news about Dottie and Brady's little baby.

"Esther Mae, I don't think we need to let you near the baby when she's born. She might have nightmares when she gets a whiff of the ten gallons of gardenia perfume you're shellacked in!"

Esther Mae's eyes widened. "I don't smell anything. I only put on three squirts."

"Three squirts!" Norma Sue barked. "That stuff is so nasty a little dab'll kill ya."

"Norma Sue, shame on you," Rose said, making Norma Sue chuckle. "You do not smell, Esther Mae. The baby is going to love you."

Norma Sue was about to tease her buddy more, but the doctor came walking through the double doors and she zeroed in on him instead. "So how is our Dottie?" she demanded. "And our baby?"

"I'm pleased to report that Dottie just gave birth to

a seven-pound twelve-ounce baby girl. Both mother and baby are doing well."

A cheer went up.

"And the daddy," Lacy called over the roar. "How's he holding up?"

"He's doing fine, too. At the moment he's holding his baby and getting to know her."

After explaining that they would be able to view the baby in a few minutes down at the baby room, he left them all.

Rose sank happily into her chair as the group charged toward the end of the hall to wait next to the glass for the baby to appear.

Lacy plopped down beside her. "Our first baby girl. What do you think?"

"I'm thrilled."

"Me, too. But I look thrilled, don't you think?" She gave an extreme grin.

Rose choked with laughter. "Yes, you look thrilled. And a bit crazy."

"Just the way it should be. *You,* on the other hand, look a million miles away. And miserable to be there."

Rose slid her friend a long-suffering look. "Why do you have to be so observant?"

"Because God made me that way. And since I do feel a little responsible for helping to set you up the other night I have to ask if some of this might have to do with a certain handsome deputy?"

Rose moaned. "You kill me. And, yes, you should be very ashamed of your part in that little setup you worked out the other night."

"That didn't answer my question at all." Lacy tapped her forehead. "Where are you right now?"

"Oh, if you must know I'm going out to Zane's this evening."

"*Really.* This is promising."

"No. I'm just going to look."

"Looking is good. Talking is better. But looking is a start. I love to look at Clint. Sometimes I just sit across from him and I just can't believe he's mine."

"Lacy! I'm going to look at his house for crying out loud."

"Seriously, Rose. Do you even know how to have a good time? I'm not joking. You do remember what that is like, don't you?"

Rose wasn't so sure if she did. She chose to ignore the question. "I'm only going because I'm trying to be amicable for Max's sake."

"Oh, brother. Are we back there so soon? We talked about this the other night. You need to do something for your sake."

"If I did something for my sake I'd stay away from Zane."

"I can't believe you," Lacy said, springing from the chair as if it were Esther Mae's mini exercise trampoline. "I'm beginning to think you are a hopeless case."

"Gee, thanks."

"Seriously. If you aren't going to go out with Zane then you need to start dating someone. Anyone."

Rose stood up, deciding this conversation needed to die a quick death. "Come on. Let's go see the baby." Esther Mae practically had her nose plastered to the glass, which was a good indication that the baby had just been wheeled out for viewing.

Lacy fell into step beside her. "On second thought, you shouldn't go out with anyone else. You should marry Zane and have another child."

"Lacy!"

"Rose!" Lacy echoed her, chuckled. "I'm just teasing you. But really go out there tonight and make me proud."

Rose groaned. "What I'm going to do is go look at this beautiful baby."

"Me, too. Then I'm going to drive you home so you can get ready for that great date."

"This is not a date," Rose reminded herself that afternoon as she drove toward Zane's. Her nerves were tingling they were so frazzled. She clearly understood too many close encounters with Zane would weaken her resolve. She'd been thinking about that all day.

Zane didn't realize that she didn't need to come out and look at his new home. She knew it well. It was a lovely mid-size ranch with beautiful old oaks spread out over the front pastures. It was the type of landscape that inspired a person to want to walk through the open fields between the trees. Especially in early April when the bluebonnets dotted the landscape like a deep blue carpet. Which was the way it looked the first time she'd come and looked at it last year.

The way it had looked the day she'd fallen in love with it.

Today, since it was practically May, the pasture was a vibrant yellow from the brown-eyed Susans that blanketed the land. Turning onto the dirt drive that was actually a private dirt road to the house, she remembered the day she'd driven back here for the first time. She'd let herself dream that she could afford to buy such a place for herself and Max. Of course she'd never told anyone. Being a realist, she had known with her meager resources it was an impossible dream.

But still, she'd come to look…often.

Like Max said, it had a cactus patch that spread for acres and acres. It was the type of natural resource that would have enabled her to stretch her business straight from the start. But it was only a dream and she'd been more than thrilled to be blessed to buy the property where they lived now. The land had been cheap and small but ideally perfect for starting her business. For giving her and Max a home within the realms of their budget. She loved her home.

Still, if she'd had the money, this would have been her true dream home. It was a secret that would go to the grave with her. And an odd irony that Zane would move here and buy it.

Of course he would though. It was the prettiest property in four counties, even if a person didn't find the prickly pear patch an extra-special feature.

The house came into view as she topped a slight hill. Just the sight of it sent a warm happy feeling through her. It was just a sprawling ranch, white with bold black shutters and a detached garage that was connected to the house with a covered patio. She knew from walking around the place and peeking in the windows that there was a flagstone patio on the back with a massive stone grill built to one side. It was a very masculine home on the interior. But she loved the simple bold lines of it and the larger scale of all things. It fit the landscape. It looked like it fit Zane.

He'd bought two pots of red geraniums at some point and they sat beside the sidewalk near the front door. A welcome splash of color against the white backdrop.

The house was actually perfect for Zane. The fact that she kept harping on that detail grated on her already frazzled nerves as she rang the doorbell.

There was no answer, so she rang it again and, after waiting a few more minutes, she walked around to the backyard.

Several yards, practically a football field's distance from the house, there was a large metal barn. She headed that way.

"Max," she called. She was halfway there when she saw Zane's truck coming from the road and behind him driving an all-terrain utility vehicle was Max. Rose's first inclination was to get angry. How dare Zane let Max drive one of those four-wheeler type vehicles!

The minute he got out of the truck she was beside him.

"What do you mean letting him drive that?"

Zane looked like she'd lost her marbles. "He's fourteen, Rose. It's a ranch vehicle."

"But—"

Max laughed as he barreled off the seat. "Mom, chill. It's as safe as a golf cart."

She wanted to say more, but realized that it was the truth. She was just being overprotective or a little territorial where Max was concerned. It was clearly something she was going to have to get over.

The fact that Max looked happy thrilled her.

"Look what I've got in the back," Max said, waving her to the small bed of the vehicle. It was no more than about three feet by three feet, maybe four, but it was absolutely packed with prickly pears.

"You picked all of that today?"

"Yes, ma'am. And there's tons more where those

came from! We're going to have plenty of jelly juice. All you have to do is sell it. I'm going to be working like a dog over the next few weeks picking and torching these babies and the rest out there waiting to be picked."

He slid onto the bench seat of the little truck and grabbed the steering wheel. "C'mon," he said, and slapped the seat beside him. "You have to see this."

Zane doffed his hat. "After you."

Rose slid onto the seat beside Max and scooted closer to him when Zane sat down on the other side of her.

"Hit the road, kiddo," he said, looking past her to Max.

"Sounds like a plan," Max called and hit the gas— the kid had ridden in Lacy's car far too many times it seemed.

Rose watched silently as he maneuvered the tiny work truck down the lane. She concentrated on watching him and not the fact that her entire right side was pressed against Zane's left side. He needed more room, naturally, and so he'd automatically put his arm across the back of the seat. His hand dangled off the back of the seat between her shoulder and Max, therefore basically placing her in his relaxed embrace. That was hard to ignore.

"I really do love the place," she said, glancing up at him. The wind was whipping all around them in the open-air vehicle and she was pretty certain she looked a sight. His hair was short and since he had on his hat he looked just as handsome as always. Life just wasn't fair sometimes.

"I'm *really* glad you do. I wouldn't have bought it if I felt you wouldn't like it."

His admission caught her off guard and the light that warmed his eyes told her he knew it.

She looked away, trying not to put too much meaning on his admission. His hand brushed her arm, sending a thrill of unwanted awareness through her. Her gaze dropped to his hand…only he wasn't caressing her arm but had simply touched her arm to draw her attention to what he was pointing to.

Embarrassed at her assumption, she looked at the pasture he was pointing at and told herself she would stop jumping to conclusions as they drove through an open gate, and crossed the pasture to where the cactus spread out before them.

"Isn't it amazing, Mom?"

She nodded, awed by the sight of the cactus just like she'd been all the other times she'd come to look.

"Max gave me a history lesson about all of this."

"He's done his homework," she said. "It's amazing to think areas like this could stretch for such long distances and also have been so important to our heritage. Not only for sustaining the Indians' lives with food but also socially and economically."

Zane glanced at her. "I like the way it looks, too. There is just something beautiful about those ugly purple tunas hanging off them."

Max giggled. *Giggled.*

Rose laughed at her son's reaction to Zane's bizarre statement and at the statement itself. It just seemed odd coming from him. But as they all three sat together on the seat of the little truck and stared out across the rolling hills covered in cactus she couldn't help but wonder if he'd made the statement because he understood. Understood the ugly purple fruit symbolized so much more to her than just a paycheck.

Could he know working with the prickly pear symbolized taking all the ugly parts of her life and turning them into something beautiful? No, no one would understand that but her.

"Let's head back, Max," he said after a minute and to Rose he said, "We thought we'd grill some burgers on the pit."

"But," she started to protest, feeling vulnerable. This was not a date. She'd only come here to look at the house and then she and Max would go home. Dinner wasn't in the bargain.

"Mom," Max said. "Don't say no. We have to celebrate Dad getting his new place. It's only right."

She counted to ten, knowing she was being ganged up on, but she couldn't take this from Max. "Burgers sound great," she said, and folded her hands in her lap as she prepared herself for what waited for her back at the house.

A very hard time, that's what it was.

She wondered if God was getting a kick out of torturing her…because it sure seemed like it to her.

Zane Cantrell was not playing fair.

Rose fumed silently as she drove home later that evening. He was letting her weakness for seeing Max happy to his advantage.

Beside her Max was quiet as he stared out the window into the darkness. He was probably sitting there basking in the wonderful evening they'd just had. Oh, and it had been wonderful.

The perfect cozy family night of burgers on the grill. Great conversation sitting at the outdoor table followed by a little stargazing as a family unit. Oh, the man was devious.

And charming and completely relentless in the fact that he was the perfect gentleman. He never made advances, never tried to kiss her...not since that day at her house had he tried to kiss her. He hadn't even made remarks that insinuated that he wanted to. But just the same, she had his number.

Zane had figured out her weakness and he was hitting her with everything he had.

"Mom," Max said, turning in his seat to look straight at her. "I can't kid you. I want that."

Ha! He didn't have to elaborate; she knew exactly what "that" was. *You want it, too.* She clamped a lid on that thought.

"But I want you to know that I'm okay with the way things are."

He nodded to reassure her as her startled gaze riveted to him. It didn't as she planted her wary gaze back on the road.

"Zane talked to me and helped me see that I need to back off with the matchmaking thing."

She inhaled sharply. "Do you mean that?"

"Yes, ma'am. Just, can we not get all territorial about it? I mean. Like tonight. Sometimes it's just nice to have dinner with both of you or maybe lunch sometimes. I mean I won't push for y'all to be a couple if y'all can just give me that sometimes."

Rose turned the car into their driveway. Was this a ploy? This idea worried her far more than his blatant attempt at matchmaking. "Are you being up front about this? Or is this another plan?"

"No plan. I promise. I just really enjoyed being like a family tonight. And the other night when Zane came over and we all looked at pictures and stuff. I like it. You have to believe me. I'm not going to lie and say

I don't wish something more would come of it, but that's between the two of you." Max looked vulnerable even though he was trying not to.

"Sure. Fair enough then," Rose said. Forcing her lips to lift, she pressed for sincere.

"Thanks, Mom. I get it now, I think. It's like the posse told me in the beginning when I begged them to help me. If the love's not there then I don't want y'all together in the first place. It would only make y'all miserable in the end and, Mom…" He hit sincere with one look, no force employed. "All I ever wanted was for you to be happy. You believe that, don't you?"

This time she smiled and her depth of sincerity matched his. "Yes, honey. I believe that with all my heart."

He reached across the car and hugged her, then hopped out and jogged inside.

Rose took a deep breath and held it for a few seconds before expelling it slowly, thoughtfully.

If the love's not there then I don't want y'all together in the first place. It would only make y'all miserable in the end.

But what if the love was there? What if the love was there but her fear was holding her back?

Rose leaned her head back and prayed for some guidance. This turmoil was horrible. The day Zane had reappeared in her life she'd been more at peace than she'd ever been in her life. She'd been on the brink of something new and life changing. She'd known what she wanted and where she wanted to go. And then Zane had shown up and shattered all that peace by reminding her of the dream she'd forced herself to forget…the dream, the heart's desire that had hurt too much to continue dreaming about.

There were all kinds of excuses she'd used over the past few weeks about why she couldn't let herself…admit, or give in to that love.

She walked toward the house and turned everything upside down in her head, in her heart… What did she want?

What did *she,* the independent woman that she needed to be, really want?

It simply wasn't something she was going to answer quickly and that might possibly be where all of her turmoil was coming from.

Chapter Nineteen

Zane liked Clint Matlock. The successful cattleman was married to Lacy. The couple was very involved in the community and pitched in and helped out wherever they were needed. His new property bordered Clint's; he'd found out last week when Clint was helping park cars at the play. He'd invited Zane to a roping at his ranch afterward, but Zane hadn't gone that night. Tonight when he'd called and invited him over Zane had come without hesitation. His house was too empty after Rose and Max left.

Getting to know Clint better and some of the other men who'd come was something he needed to do. His life was different now…he needed to learn that there was more than work.

He'd always lived a life where his duty ruled, where his focus was about making sure other people lived to *live* their lives. And he hadn't had much of one. At the end of the day he'd always gone home to an empty house. *When* he'd gone home. He'd lived much of the time on the road.

"Hey, you look like you're a hundred miles away,"

Clint said, reining his horse in beside where Zane was standing.

Zane shrugged. "Actually, I was only about ten miles away."

Clint folded his hands over the saddle horn and gave him a knowing look. "Lacy is pretty excited about you and Rose."

"I wish Rose was excited about it."

"So, there's a problem?"

"A big one." Zane propped a boot on the bottom fence rung and rested an elbow on the upper rung. He took a moment to study the night sky where the blinking red light of an airplane moved, seemingly from one star to the next. "I'm in over my head, I think."

"I'm sure it's been hard finding out all these years you had a son."

Most of the other men were leading their horses to their trailers and calling it a night and for a minute Zane was tempted to head out, too. "Yeah, but now that I know, all I can think of is making up for lost time."

"I can imagine. But Rose isn't seeing it the same way?"

"Nope. She doesn't trust me. I think she wants to. But, you know, her life has been tough. I've failed her in every sense of the word." He wasn't one to open up to people, but he needed a sounding board and Clint seemed as solid as they came.

Clint's saddle creaked as he shifted his weight and studied him hard. "Then don't fail her again. Simple as that."

"Right," he said, regretting that he'd said anything.

Clint laughed and hauled himself out of the saddle. "Man, don't look so stewed over. Yeah, I know that sounds like one of those stupid patronizations. I hate those things. If you notice I didn't tell you to go pray about it."

Zane chuckled. "Yeah, well, that's a relief." It was a given that he'd been praying plenty, so someone telling him to pray wouldn't have been a welcomed comment.

Clint dropped his reins and his big bay dropped his head and plucked around for grass. "All I'm saying is, you can only start fresh. You can't keep looking back and beating yourself up over the past. You need to go after what you want. Maybe state your case point-blank so there's no misunderstanding of what you want. And then sit back and be patient."

Zane thought about that for a minute. It was good.

"Buying that piece of property couldn't have hurt any, either."

"How so?" Zane asked, catching the gleam in Clint's eyes.

"Oh, the family who owned it have been after me to buy it ever since they moved away. But I didn't need that big house sitting square in the center of all that land…but mostly I didn't need that swath of prickly pear that stretches across who knows how many acres." He cocked a knowing brow.

Zane grinned. "What can I say? I need everything I can get to win brownie points."

Clint clapped him on the back. "I'm not sure I've ever heard of a man using prickly pear cactus for brownie points but in your case it just might work."

Zane wasn't so sure about that. But as he drove home he thought about everything Clint had said. Especially the part about stating his case point-blank so there was no misunderstandings and then being patient. The house had been a subtle hint to her.

She'd said she liked the place. She liked the giant oaks that dotted the land and she'd said the sprawling ranch house had character. That had been enough for him to buy the place.

He was going to load the deck in his favor any way he could. He wanted Rose and Max in his life. She had a wall built around her heart…he wasn't sure if it was there against any cowboy who showed up vying for it or if it was just him. But one thing he did know—God willing, he was going to do everything in his power to be the one who tore them down.

And in the process he was going to have to tear down a few of his own. Nothing about it was going to be easy. He pulled up in front of his house and got out. Yeah, it had been a subtle declaration of what he wanted.

But maybe the time for subtlety was over. Maybe it was time to make his intentions perfectly clear.

Rose was standing inside the window display of Ashby's Treasures changing out the dresses. The shop had been busy all morning—a regular revolving door as everyone came to find out how she'd enjoyed herself out at Zane's. Word traveled entirely too quickly in a small town. Even App and Stanley had ambled over to find out how it went—she'd had a hamburger at Zane's house and suddenly everyone practically had them married off!

She'd given up trying to tone down everyone's excitement for now, but she was going to have to figure something out. No matter what Max had said last night she knew he secretly still had hopes that she and Zane would end up together. She'd seen it in his eyes and heard it in his voice. She knew her son well.

Zane was fighting dirty.

She pulled another pin from between her lips and was jamming it into the sill when a flash of color caught her eye. Looking up, she saw Zane coming down the street—holding a bouquet of brightly colored flowers!

She watched, transfixed as he started across the street and headed straight for her. "No! No! No!"

Pretty sure steam was boiling out of her ears, she dropped the netting and the pins and hurried out of the window. She was going to kill him!

She met him on the sidewalk. "What are you doing?"

He tipped his hat; his beautiful eyes twinkled. "Don't look so alarmed. Can't a cowboy bring a woman flowers?"

"No! He most certainly cannot and you very well know it." This wasn't good. Not at all. He looked too wonderful. Too tempting.

He faked shock as he pulled the summer bouquet close to his chest. "Why?" he asked.

"You just can't. Max started getting false hope again last night. I saw it. And now this. Parading down Main Street with those." She stared at the flowers. They were absolutely beautiful. Bright and lovely. Happy flowers. "Max will surely hear about this—" Pete was loading feed across the street and had stopped to stare. And no doubt App and Stanley were getting an eyeful from their window at the diner.

"So?"

"So! This is unacceptable. Not only he, but everyone is going to think we're…that there is something going on between us. They already think it—"

"And why exactly would that be a bad thing? Tell me, Rose."

She faltered. "Because." She hesitated. "Because there isn't. I thought we understood each other. I can't."

Zane reached for her arm and lifted her hand then laid the flowers across her limp palm. "Take them. Toss them in the trash after I leave if you want. But here's the deal, Rose." He gently folded her fingers around the stems, holding her gaze captive with his own.

"I've been going back and forth in my head about the best thing for a guy in love to do. And here's the thing. Fourteen years ago, we had something. Something real, something worthwhile between us. And I messed up. Today, I can't pretend anymore that I don't care. And I can't lie to my son and tell him I just want to be friends with his mom. I'm giving you notice that I'm about to go after something I want. Something I've wanted all these years."

"No, don't do this."

"Too late. I'm doing it." He stepped close, dipped his chin and hit her with unnervingly serious eyes. "I want you, Rose Vincent. I want you in my life. I want you as my wife. I love you like no man has ever loved a woman and I want you to give us a fighting chance."

Her heart was pounding. She knew he could feel her pulse beneath his fingertips. Very slowly he rubbed his thumb across the beat and gave her a tender smile. Her fingers automatically curled around the flowers so she wouldn't drop them. As much as she was disturbed she was also intrigued…and breathless. Thrilled. He loved her.

"I'm not going to push. But we've wasted enough time and I don't want to waste another minute. I'm stating my facts just so you know."

Zane's tender words, so sure, so determined, wrapped around her bruised heart and a dangerous hope sprung inside of her.

She couldn't speak as he brushed his lips across hers, tipped his hat and left.

She touched her fingertips to her lips and took a shallow breath—it did nothing to settle her emotions. Staring down at the flowers, all she could wonder was what was she going to do now?

No sooner had Zane disappeared inside Sam's than Lacy and Sheri came busting through her door from the hair salon. Sheri was brandishing a red-tipped nail polish brush.

"So spill," Lacy said.

"Now," Sheri demanded.

"He brought me flowers."

"*And,*" Lacy said, dragging the word out with a grin.

"And what?" she asked. "I don't want flowers from him."

Sheri laughed. "Yeah, right."

"I don't. Do you know what this will do to Max if he finds out... I can't believe Zane just marched down Main Street like he was God's gift to women!"

Lacy and Sheri looked at each other like they knew a secret that she didn't know. "Stop looking like that," Rose demanded. "I'll never hear the end of this when Norma Sue and the others find out."

"Yep, you do have a point," Lacy said, totally faking her concern. Rose could tell they were both thrilled. "So what does the card say?"

The card. Reading it hadn't crossed her mind. Now she stared at it.

"You look like you're afraid of it," Lacy said, concern replaced her teasing.

"I am a little."

"Love is a scary thing," Sheri said. "But wonderful. Open it." She pointed the nail brush at the card.

"I'm not—"

Sheri held up a hand. "Save it for someone else."

"C'mon," Lacy said, nudging her in the arm. "This is exciting. If you don't open it, I will."

Rose handed the flowers to Lacy before pulling the small white card from the envelope.

I'll be waiting...Zane. She recognized his handwriting immediately. He'd written the card after the flowers were delivered instead of letting the florist write it for him at the shop.

"Ah, that's sweet," Lacy said.

Sheri leaned in to read his words again. "Clearly, the ball is officially in your court."

"This is good—"

"No, Lacy, it isn't," Rose whispered and took a shuddering breath. "I want him to have a life with Max...but I think it's too late for us to go back."

"Why?" Lacy handed her back the flowers. The orange and pink daisies stared up at her.

"Because I don't trust the feelings I have with him or with anyone, really. My life was just starting to make sense before he showed up. I was finally feeling in control. And I'm not willing to risk messing it up because I make a bad choice. Does that make sense?" She wasn't sure anymore.

"Oh, Rose," Lacy said, hugging her. "Don't look so sad. Knowing what you've been through, it makes perfect sense."

"But who knows what will be," Sheri said. She was

smiling. "It won't hurt for Zane to prove to you that he's not a bad choice. He's willing to wait."

"That's right," Lacy agreed. "Maybe if he works at it hard enough he'll change your mind." She raised an eyebrow.

Rose didn't want him to try to change her mind. She was afraid of him trying; despite all of her talk, she didn't feel very strong where he was concerned. All night at dinner, she kept imagining them as a family. That it was wonderful… It wasn't that she didn't like the feelings he evoked, she just didn't trust them. Too much had happened to her to trust that she wouldn't get hurt again. She didn't want to give away control of her state of mind—of her heart.

Did she?

She had to stay strong. Easier said than done. Every time she saw him, her emotions and feelings tangled irrationally. And that was it right there—how could she trust feelings like that?

Sheri pulled open the door. "I better go back and finish painting Mrs. Carver's toes. Keep us posted."

"I better go, too," Lacy said, and then hugged Rose. "Just so you know. I'm praying that God works everything in your life out and that He eases your mind. When things are right there is a peace that He gives you that won't let you down."

Rose sighed. "That's why I'm so confused right now. I'd almost reached that peaceful place and then Zane waltzed back into my life and wiped it out."

"All I can tell you is there's a reason for everything. We just don't always see it. I know it gets old hearing that, but it's true."

She watched Lacy jog down the sidewalk then closed the door and found a vase in the back for Zane's flowers. She'd be lying if she didn't admit that part of her was touched by the beautiful bouquet and she wasn't about to let them die before their time.

Chapter Twenty

The week's normal routine started the next morning. She went to work, but drove Max out to Zane's so that he could harvest prickly pear. To her relief Zane checked on him off and on during the day and usually brought him home so that she didn't keep having to drive out there. Which meant she didn't have to worry so much about the pressures she sensed there. The pressure of wanting the life there on that beautiful land in that lovely house…making it a home for her and Max with Zane.

But she had to hand it to Zane, he was going out of his way to take that stress off her. And she appreciated it.

She thought. He was also conspicuously not saying anything else about the flowers or his feelings. And neither was Max, who she was quite certain had heard every little detail about what his dad had done.

It was a conspiracy. And she was trying to ignore it and just make the situation as normal as she could.

"So you're going to hear about the loan on Monday?" Ashby asked on Friday.

"Yes, and I'm terrified."

Ashby looked up from the computer screen. "There is no reason for that. Yes, you have blank spots in your credit history but I don't think that's going to come into play with this loan. It's too far back. You have great references, a solid business plan and the most recent credit history you have is excellent. I honestly don't believe you're going to be turned down. But if by some chance you are, I'm telling you all I have to do is make a call and my banker will give it to you. I promise."

"Thank you, but you know how much I want to do this on my own."

"Yes, and I applaud that. But, Rose, this is business and it is common practice. Sometimes even the big names got their start because they borrowed money from friends, family or through bank loans that originated because of who they knew. If you get turned down—and really I'm speaking as your friend and as your business mentor—if you get turned down and you let your pride keep you from taking what your connections offer you then you are making a grave mistake. Connections are gold in business. How do you think I got my start? Yes, I had wealthy parents but I still needed start-up capital. I wasn't going to shoot myself in the foot by turning my back on what my friends could help me with. Pride can be your worst enemy sometimes."

Rose respected Ashby so much. She'd built a very exclusive high-end dress store in San Francisco, but she'd created an even stronger online presence, which had enabled her to close her store in San Francisco and relocate to this tiny town. The smaller boutique here generated more entertainment than profit. But, like she was saying, it all started because she let her business mind rule and not her heart.

Ashby and Dottie had both taught Rose about running a business and she really felt like she could make a go of it, but first she had to get over her pride and get the expansion loan.

"Thank you," she said. "I promise, if I don't get the loan on my own merit I will use every connection I have to make this dream a reality."

"Good. I'm going to hold you to it. Now, on the personal side, how are you holding up?"

She tried not to frown. "Pretty good. I'm struggling a bit with myself."

"How so?"

She paused slipping a dress on a hanger. "Am I making this too hard? You know, like I am with this loan. Part of me wants to hold on to my independence. Part of me thinks I'm just scared and using that as something to hide behind. And part of me says just trust my heart and do the easy thing."

Ashby laughed. "The easy thing. What about any of that is the easy thing?"

"Giving in and marrying Zane. Being a family. Making Max happy. That would be the easy thing."

Ashby came around the counter and hugged her tightly. "I really get it," she said when they broke apart.

"You do? Because, believe me, I'm not totally sure that I do."

"You don't want to do the wrong thing. You don't want to do the easy thing. You want to do the right thing. It is as simple as that. And until you know the right thing, you are holding your ground...because that is the right thing to do until you know otherwise."

Rose looked at Ashby in amazement. "You make it sound so simple."

"I might make it sound that way, but I know matters of the heart aren't simple at all. Oh, Rose." She laid her hand on her flat stomach. "I'm going to have a baby. I've dreamed of a baby for so long. But getting here in my life wasn't easy for me either. You were there for me when I fought falling in love with Dan. You know it took me a while to come to my conclusions about what I wanted and who I wanted. But I did eventually. And so will you."

"I hope you're right."

"You'll know. And speaking of that, looks like you've got company."

Rose turned to see Zane and Max climbing out of Zane's truck. They were smiling when they walked inside.

"Hey, Mom," Max said. "We're having lunch over at Sam's place. Do you want to come?"

Zane stood just inside the door and had taken his hat off and was holding it across his heart as he was prone to do. Her gaze lingered on the corded strength of his forearm and on the hand that rested over the top of the hat. She swallowed hard and glanced at Ashby, who gave her a knowing smile.

"I'll hold the fort down. You go have lunch with your son." Ashby put no emphasis on the word *son* but Rose understood what she was saying. Have lunch with them for Max. Relax.

"Okay," Rose said. Zane immediately pulled the door open and held it for her and Max to pass. Ashby mouthed the word *relax* when she glanced back at her and Rose took a deep breath as she walked beside Zane. The strangest thing happened as they walked and she listened to Max talk about his morning…she didn't have to force herself to relax. She *was* relaxed.

And she stayed that way through the entire meal. She and Zane sat on opposite sides of the booth, which was probably part of it. She was accepting that her nerves going ballistic because he was so near was normal. Looking at him acting so…calm, one would never suspect that this was the man who'd given her flowers and told her that he loved her.

He was waiting. Just like Max was. She should be aggravated about the whole thing and she had been…but her anger had sunk into the background, replaced with this honest confusion.

She loved watching him and Max together. They had become so comfortable, she realized as she watched them. When Zane had first come into their lives, she'd felt jealousy when he spent time with his dad. That was gone, replaced with a genuine appreciation and enjoyment for the relationship they had developed.

She was finishing up the last of her fries when this dawned on her and she paused, looking down at the fry she'd just dipped in ketchup, and gave God a much-deserved thank-you. When she looked up, Zane was watching her. She smiled and he reciprocated with a thoughtful one of his own.

"Would it be okay with you if Max spent the night out at my place tonight?"

"Oh." The question caught her off guard for some strange reason. "Sure."

"Thanks, Mom." Max plopped a fry into his mouth. "We're going camping. Gil's coming, too. I already called him but told him it depended on if you gave us the okay."

"Sounds like fun."

Max on a campout with his dad. Her heart swelled with a gladness that felt like it would explode.

"You're welcome to come," Zane said. Beside him Max gave her an enthusiastic nod.

"Oh, no," she said. "This sounds like a male bonding thing. A girl would just get in the way."

"You're never in the way, Rose," Zane said, his voice gravelly and his golden eyes darkened in a way that sent a thrill bouncing through her.

She laughed, nervous in an instant.

"Come on, Mom. It'll be fun."

"You're not afraid, are you?" Zane asked.

She knew there was more to the question than asking about a camping trip.

You're not afraid, are you?

She lifted her chin and met his challenging gaze straight on. "I'm not afraid."

His lips curled slowly. "Then you'll go?"

"Yes, I'll go," she said, feeling a sense of anticipation at the idea of going camping with her son and his dad. Was she saying yes to more?

"Now we're talking," Max yelped and rammed a fist into the air, causing her and Zane to laugh. Their gazes locked just as his emergency beeper buzzed to life.

Chapter Twenty-One

Zane glanced down at the number on the beeper. "Excuse me," he said, and walked through the diner to the counter.

Rose watched him ask Sam to borrow his phone. Mule Hollow was in a dead zone and not much cell-phone service made it through, so landlines were still essential. Small-town life had some drawbacks and most of the time lack of cell-phone service wasn't much of an issue. But in an emergency every moment counted. As Zane strode around the counter and snatched up the phone, a sense of foreboding overcame Rose. Nothing ever happened in Mule Hollow, though she didn't feel reassured by the knowledge.

"What do you think it is?" Max asked as he watched Zane talking on the phone.

"I don't know. I'm sure it's nothing too bad." Brady was back in town and, true to her word, Dottie had sent him back to work immediately. Zane and Brady were sharing the duties again. She'd talked with Brady the day before when he'd stopped by the shop to buy Dottie a gift. He was as happy a man as there ever was.

She wondered if it was him on the other end of the line or if it was the 911 dispatch they shared with the surrounding county.

Within seconds Zane was back and Rose knew before he spoke a word that something bad had happened. There was a keen alertness to his eyes—eyes that had seen it all and were determined to fix it. Every purposeful step he took was filled with intent. As he approached she recognized it all from...*before*.

Rose's heart caught in her chest—this was the man who'd walked into the room where a scared young woman sat completely uncertain about what her next move should be. Rose remembered how terrified she'd been after seeing the murder. She'd gone to the police because she hadn't known what else to do. Fear had taken her there...not heroics. But *this* was the Texas Ranger who'd looked into her eyes and in that single intense exchange inspired her to be brave.

Until this moment, Rose hadn't fully comprehended that she'd stepped up to the plate to see justice served because Texas Ranger Zane Cantrell's gaze made her want to be the very best form of herself that she could possibly be. But it was the absolute, undeniable truth. And as he came to a halt at her table and settled his gaze on her she understood it.

"I've got to go," he said, breaking into her revelation. "That was Brady. A vehicle matching the description of one suspected of being used in a bank robbery and hostage abduction of a three-year-old in Kerrville was spotted turning off the highway a few minutes ago. We're setting up a roadblock and checkpoint at the crossroads."

Rose's hand went to her throat and she nodded. "We'll pray," she said and held his gaze for a moment before he touched Max's shoulder and then strode toward the door.

"Can I help, Dad?" Max called as they stood.

Zane spun. "Sorry, son." He looked around the room. Cowboys all over the diner had risen and App and Stanley had, too. Even at their age, like the war veterans that they were, they looked ready to take on the world.

"Can we help?" App asked and echoes came from others.

"Please," Zane said, holding up a hand. "Everyone stay. They wounded a bank teller and are armed and dangerous. For this child's sake I need all of you to stay away from the crossroads."

"You got it," Sam said, stepping to the front of the room. "Godspeed to you, Zane."

Zane nodded and then he was gone.

Everyone was silent as they followed him outside and watched him climb into his truck, and a moment later he was gone.

Max wrapped an arm around Rose's waist and hugged her to his hip. "Don't worry, Mom. I can tell you this. If that little girl is in that car, *my dad* will get her back."

Rose draped her arm about his shoulders and hugged him closer. "Yes, he will," she said with complete certainty that he would...or would die trying.

Watching him leave, Rose had never felt more clarity about what she wanted than in that moment. But was it too late?

Zane worked on adrenaline as he raced toward the roadblock point. He knew he had the Texas highway patrol converging from all directions and air support

on the way. Brady was on the way also, but had been
at home, which would put him behind Zane. Zane
figured he was the first in a direct path to meet the
suspects.

A little girl's safety hung in the balance. Zane
prayed for God's deliverance of her and focused on his
job. On the skills that had made him the Ranger who'd
believed he'd been put on earth for a purpose to fight
for those who couldn't fight for themselves...he'd lost
faith in that to an extent after he'd stepped over the line
with Rose. And even though he'd become a believer
after his accident he hadn't ever completely gotten that
feeling back. Self-respect lost played with a man's
head.

But he knew as he headed down the road that God
had equipped him and placed him in this spot, in this
moment out here in the middle of nowhere, for a
reason and it was barreling down the road toward
him...and Zane had no intention of messing up. Of
letting that baby down. Running on instinct and something more, Zane kept going when he hit the crossroads where he was supposed to set up the roadblock.
The crossroads was nine miles from Mule Hollow and
fifty miles from the highway. Brady would set the
roadblock up, but Zane was in an unmarked vehicle
and something told him he could use that to his advantage.

He tugged his badge off and dropped it in his shirt
pocket as he slowed to an unsuspicious rate of speed.

The radio barked to life. "Zane, where are you?"

Brady. Zane snatched up the handset. "I'm twenty
miles between the crossroads and the highway." There
was a pause, and he knew Brady was fighting the urge
to reprimand. But Zane had already realized that Brady

wasn't a man who wasted time on water under the bridge.

"You see anything?" he asked finally.

"No, wait. I see it. They're on the side of the road. Looks like a flat. I'm going in."

"Zane—"

He clicked the radio off. He didn't need it barking and giving away his advantage.

He had the element of surprise going for him. He couldn't believe they were sitting on the side of the road with a flat. *A flat.*

But he wasn't griping. And he wasn't hesitating. He knew instantly how to react. He pulled over, intentionally leaving a distance between him and the car. "You boys need some help?" he called, sticking his head out the window and smiling like a good ol' boy with no clue as to who they were or what they'd done.

The two men took him at face value, assuming he was just a dumb cowboy doing the neighborly thing. Zane knew they were desperate and as such he'd expected they would pretend to accept his help. He hadn't missed the flash of steel when he'd driven up or that each held his right hand slightly behind him as they approached. They would jack his truck, kill him if they had to. He read it in their eyes that they'd crossed the line of caring anything about human life. He bided his time and willed them to keep coming away from the car, where he saw a small blond head peeking from the backseat.

He had God on his side as they approached his truck, moving away from the car and the toddler.

"Thanks for stopping, man," one said, smiling. They held their guns hidden behind them fully intent on pulling them out the instant they were beside him.

Zane let them come. The last thing they expected was the gun leveled on them the instant they came to a halt.

Zane had been in life-and-death situations numerous times over the years and never had he seen something with so much potential to end badly be resolved so easily.

"I'll take those guns," he said, with steel in his voice and his eyes. He had no compulsion to do what was needed to make certain that little girl got home to her parents. "Slow and easy on the ground there."

Within seconds of him stepping out of his truck and their palms flat against the hood of his truck, all manner of sirens and flashing lights broke loose.

Zane understood without a doubt that God had been in control of this situation. If he'd been in his marked vehicle, or if any hint of sirens or lights had come a second earlier, his window of surprise would have been lost.

God's timing had been perfect.

Zane sent up a heartfelt prayer of thanks and later as he watched the helicopter lift off with the little girl headed for home, his heart was at peace. He was glad to see the news helicopters leave, along with the police chopper.

"You ready to go?" Brady asked, a grin plastered to his face. "B'cause I know I am. I have a wife to hug and a baby of my own to hold. You did good, Zane."

"I did my job."

"Yeah, I know." He clapped him on the shoulder.

Zane knew he understood. Brady had been on the Houston police force before returning to his hometown to become sheriff. Zane knew he'd seen his share of unhappy endings and understood how wrong this one could have turned out. Zane wanted to go home and hug his family, too. And, God willing, he would.

The first thing he noticed as he followed Brady down Main Street were the cars and trucks lining every parking space and, behind them, the crowd strung out down the sidewalks. "What in the world?" he said out loud. Brady stopped in the center of the street and Zane did the same. Immediately a cheer went up and everyone rushed off the sidewalk and gathered round them. Amazed and uncertain he climbed from the truck and looked at the people he'd come to think of as friends over the past few weeks. In the front of the group stood Rose and Max.

This was his town. His people. His family. How strange God worked, he realized. When he'd driven into town he'd been a loner, closed off emotionally from everyone around him. A man who'd lived his life only for his profession. And now, God had given him such a miraculous gift by bringing him here and giving him everything.

Realization fully hit him of how God's timing had been so perfect not only in the rescue of the little girl. One tiny second off and there could have been a gunfight and she might have been shot in the crossfire. But in God's careful precise timing He'd put Zane exactly where he was supposed to be. There would be those who would say it all happened by chance, but Zane knew differently. Just as he suddenly knew it was the same with his life.

As clearly as he knew he belonged in this town and with the woman whose gaze he was riveted to. He knew God had brought him to this point in His perfect timing. He didn't understand everything but he knew there was no happenstance about it.

Rose Vincent was the only woman he would ever love. And though he hated the thought of all those years between them wasted and all the years he'd missed seeing Max grow up, Zane trusted God to bring it all together.

"You're a hero," Max said, breaking out of the pack and engulfing him in a bear hug. "It's all over the television."

Zane hugged his son tightly and met Rose's gaze over the top of his head. She had tears in her eyes as she stepped up and laid her hand on his cheek.

"We were just doing our job," he said gruffly. His heart pounded at her touch and the precious gift of having Max's arms around him. He'd never had anything like this before.

Rose smiled and brushed her thumb across his cheek. "Of course you were," she said. And the light that shone in her eyes took his breath away. There was an entire town standing around and while he was thankful for the situation having ended so well all he could really think about right now was the look in Rose's eyes and the sweet touch of her hand on his cheek.

"Can I have a word with you?"

She nodded.

"Whatcha got to say?" Applegate called, giving Zane a piercing look that asked if he was about to be smart and do everything in his power to win Rose's heart.

Zane returned App's stare with a warm one of his own. Smart man. "I'm sure you'll know directly. But for the moment I'd like to be alone."

"Sounds like a plan to me," Max said, grinning up at him.

Zane took Rose's hand and she came willingly. All he could think of was that she'd touched his cheek so gently and in her eyes he saw what he dared to hope was his future.

"Use the store," Ashby said.

"And take all the time y'all need," Norma Sue encouraged.

"That's right," Esther Mae called. "We'll be out here waiting to celebrate some more if the two of you have come to your senses."

Max put one hand on Zane's arm and one on Rose's and pushed then gently in the direction of Ashby's Treasures. "Go on," he said. "There's only one way I want this day to end."

Rose chuckled and pulled Zane into the store and closed the door behind them. Max turned his back on them and crossed his arms as if guarding the world from intruding on them. Zane knew it was the other way around. Max was blocking their path of escaping the store until he got his happy ending.

"I—" Rose began just as Zane did the same. They ended up halting their words and just staring at each other. Rose had so much she wanted to say. So much she wanted to make up for.

"Oh, Zane," she began again and he let her speak. "I've been so slow to understanding. But the minute I saw you hang that phone up in Sam's earlier and I saw that look in your eyes everything clicked into place." She stepped close and cupped his face between her hands. "I realized that no matter how our lives had gotten mixed up over the years, or what the path was that got us from that first moment when I laid eyes on you to that moment in Sam's, that I loved you because you inspire me to be strong. To be brave. To do what I must in the face of any adversity. And suddenly I understood why you walked away from me."

He pulled her close and buried his face in her neck and she felt him tremble as he held her so tightly their hearts pounded against each other. "I was so afraid of losing you," he whispered against her ear. "I would have done anything to keep you safe."

"Even give me up," she whispered and he nodded into her hair.

"I know now it was wrong. That I was too close to the case to think clearly," he said. "But I realized something this afternoon, too." He pulled back and looked into her eyes. "I realized that God in His perfect timing has brought us full circle and has put us exactly where we were meant to be."

She nodded and tears glistened in her beautiful eyes. "I know I feel the same way. I love this tiny town. And Max does, too. When I think about the path it took to bring us here it's amazing to me…and yet, this is home. And you being here has made it perfect. I'm stubborn, and a little worried that it won't be completely easy to drop the barriers I've built around my heart—"

"I like the stubborn you," Zane said softly, smoothing the hair off her forehead and kissing her temple. "And you will drop the barriers when the time is right. I'm here to stay, Rose. You don't ever have to worry that I'll be walking away again. I love you so much. And Max, what a gift…"

Rose felt so safe, so at peace.

Zane stepped back and smiled as he bent down on

one knee. Rose's heart stilled, watching him. And from outside she heard a whoop of joy and knew Max was watching, too.

"Rose, will you marry me? Will you make me the happiest man alive and spend the rest of your life with me?"

Her heart slowly started to thump, as if she were feeling it for the first time. She swallowed, but her voice wasn't working.

Zane's lips quirked at the edges. "I'm going to spend my life waiting right here on my knee if you don't say yes."

She nodded; lifting her eyes, she saw Max smiling through the glass. Tears came then and her voice, too. "Yes," she said, looking at Zane. "I've wanted this for so long."

Laughing, Zane scooped her up in a hug and kissed her finally with a passion she knew would last a life-time…and as simple as that her world was right—the shop door flew open.

"So does this mean I get my happily-ever-after?" Max asked, rushing them.

Simultaneously Zane and Rose each lifted an arm and let him into their embrace.

Zane looked into Rose's eyes and smiled. "What do you think?" he asked her, his voice a low rumble that sent her heart thundering with anticipation.

Feeling like she would burst with happiness, she looked from Zane to Max and knew her world was forever complete. "I think," she said softly, "'They lived happily ever after' sounds like the perfect begin-ning to me. Not the ending."

"Sweet!" Max whooped. "Y'all continue on. I gotta

go invite everybody to a wedding," he said and spun away; running to the door, he yelled the news to the waiting crowd.

Clapping erupted instantly, as did a stampede.

Zane chuckled against her temple. "I like this beginning."

Rose melted. "So do I," she sighed happily. "So do I."

* * * * *

Watch for Debra Clopton's next
Steeple Hill Love Inspired.
LONE STAR CINDERELLA promises to
sweep you off your feet!
Coming July 2009 from Steeple Hill Books.

Dear Reader,

Thank you for spending a few hours in Mule Hollow with me and all the gang! I had a blast working on this book because of the lighter aspects of it.

But Rose and Zane had a very complicated background, and as hard as it was for them to overcome it I really *loved* creating it.

Why? Because we all live complicated lives. Lives that are formed by our past, in a good way or a bad way. I believe we must embrace today and use our past, be it good or be it bad, to make us stronger. If we don't then we aren't helping ourselves and we certainly aren't helping God's purpose for our lives. I loved writing about Rose and how she strove to do this, even though she made mistakes along the way. Making mistakes is part of the growth process even as adults.

I pray that you will embrace your life today. And that you will allow God to have the victory in your life, to help you draw strength from Him if you are feeling weak.

I love hearing from readers. Drop by my Web site, www.debraclopton.com, and send me a note, or send me a letter at Debra Clopton, P.O. Box 1125, Madisonville, Texas 77864.

Until next time, live, laugh and trust God with all your hearts!

Debra Clopton

P.S. In June of 2009, don't miss my novella in the *Small-Town Brides* anthology—I'll be sharing the spotlight with the wonderful and talented Janet Tronstad! Wedding bells are going to ring for two cousins in Dry Creek, Montana, *and* Mule Hollow, Texas!

QUESTIONS FOR DISCUSSION

1. Did you enjoy this book? If so, why?

2. When Rose witnessed a murder, she made a choice to stand up for what she believed to be right. I've always been intrigued by the witness protection program and have thought how hard it must be for law-abiding citizens to have to enter the program. To leave behind most of their family and all of their friends, never to have contact with them again, is asking the unthinkable to me. Can you imagine how alone Rose or an actual living person must feel in that situation? Given the choice, and knowing what it would cost you, would you have come forward and volunteered to testify?

3. Zane is a man who looks at the world in black and white or wrong and right. For him there is no gray area. He feels he failed Rose when he crossed the line between professional and personal. What do you think about his belief and his behavior?

4. In the beginning of the book, Rose believes that though her life has been hard, God has led her to Mule Hollow. She is happy and Max is happy, and she believes she is exactly where God wants her to be. And yet you sense that there is some unfinished business from her past. Do you think you can be in the place God wants you to be and yet feel this way?

5. Rose's unfinished business has to do with a secret that could change her life. Do you think she had valid reasons for keeping the secret? Or do you believe that no matter what she was going through, she should have found Zane right away and told him about their baby? How do you feel about secrets?

6. There are many moral issues in this book. Did any resonate with you? List and discuss them, and how you feel about them, if you want to share with the group.

7. Zane left after the assassination attempt on Rose. What were his reasons for leaving? What are your thoughts on his motivations?

8. Rose has told herself that Max didn't need to know his father. But when Zane comes to town, she must face the reality of her decisions. Discuss this. Also, do you have areas in your life that you are in denial about?

9. Rose believes God has a plan for her life—even that He is using the hardships to teach her lessons. Do you believe this?

10. Despite Rose telling Zane she was responsible for her choices and her actions, he still feels responsible and refuses to believe otherwise. What do you think?

11. Just when you think Rose and Zane could find

happiness, we realize that Rose has another issue that comes from her past—she has a real fear of giving up her independence again. Why? And do you understand this?

12. As a widow for almost six years now, I find this issue of having to be strong and striving hard to be self-sufficient to be a personal issue. On the one hand, like Rose, we single women must embrace this independence to survive…and yet we must also rely on God. If you find yourself in a similar situation for various reasons, do you find it easy to rely on God but hard to think about how this will affect you when God sends the right man into your life? Please discuss and share your thoughts and feelings with your friends.

13. When talking with Max about protecting Rose's heart, Zane quotes *1 Corinthians* 13:4–7. It reads, "Love is patient, love is kind. It does not envy, it does not boast, it is not proud. It is not rude, it is not self-seeking, it is not easily angered, it keeps no record of wrongs. Love does not delight in evil but rejoices with the truth. It always protects, always trusts, always hopes, always perseveres." Do you believe this verse and apply it to those you love? Do you believe that understanding this verse is the key to Zane understanding and appreciating the strong, yet fragile woman Rose has become?

14. What does the prickly pear represent to Rose?

15. When Rose and Ashby are talking near the end of

the book, Rose admits that it would be easy for her, at that point, to forget the past and do the easy thing, which is to marry Zane and give Max the family he wants. What is she afraid of?

16. Does Rose believe Max was a mistake? Or does she believe he's the best thing that has ever happened to her? What are your thoughts on this?

17. What did you take away from this book? Or what did you like best about his book?

* * * * *

Turn the page for a sneak peek of Shirlee McCoy's
suspense-filled story,
THE DEFENDER'S DUTY.
On sale in May 2009 from Steeple Hill
Love Inspired Suspense.

After weeks in intensive care, police officer Jude Sinclair is finally recovering from the hit-and-run accident that nearly cost him his life. But was it an accident after all? Jude has his doubts—which get stronger when he spots a familiar black car outside his house: the same kind that accelerated before running him down two months ago. Whoever wants him dead hasn't given up, and anyone close to Jude is in danger. Especially Lacey Carmichael, the stubborn, beautiful home-care aide who refuses to leave his side, even if it means following him into danger....

"We don't have time for an argument," Jude said. "Take a look outside. What do you see?"

Lacey looked and shrugged. "The parking lot."

"Can you see your car?"

"Sure. It's parked under the streetlight. Why?"

"See the car to its left?"

"Yeah. It's a black sedan." Her heart skipped a beat as she said the words, and she leaned closer to the glass. "You don't think that's the same car you saw at the house tonight, do you?"

"I don't know, but I'm going to find out."

Lacey scooped up the grilled-cheese sandwich and shoved it into the carryout bag. "Let's go."

He eyed her for a moment, his jaw set, his gaze hot. "*We're* not going anywhere. You are staying here. I am going to talk to the driver of that car."

"I think we've been down this road before and I'm pretty sure we both know where it leads."

"It leads to you getting fired. Stay put until I get back, or forget about having a place of your own for a month." He stood and limped away, not even giving

Lacey a second glance as he crossed the room and headed into the diner's kitchen area.

Probably heading for a back door.

Lacey gave him a one-minute head start and then followed, the hair on the back of her neck standing on end and issuing a warning she couldn't ignore. Danger. It was somewhere close by again, and there was no way she was going to let Jude walk into it alone. If he fired her, so be it. As a matter of fact, if he fired her, it might be for the best. Jude wasn't the kind of client she was used to working for. Sure, there'd been other young men, but none of them had seemed quite as vital or alive as Jude. He didn't seem to need her, and Lacey didn't want to be where she wasn't needed. On the other hand, she'd felt absolutely certain moving to Lynchburg was what God wanted her to do.

"So, which is it, Lord? Right or wrong?" She whispered the words as she slipped into the diner's hot kitchen. A cook glared at her, but she ignored him. Until she knew for sure why God had brought her to Lynchburg, Lacey could only do what she'd been paid to do—make sure Jude was okay.

With that in mind, she crossed the room, heading for the exit and the client that she was sure was going to be a lot more trouble than she'd anticipated when she'd accepted the job.

Jude eased around the corner of the restaurant, the dark alleyway offering him perfect cover as he peered into the parking lot. The car he'd spotted through the window of the restaurant was still parked beside Lacey's. Black. Four door. Honda. It matched the one that had pulled up in front of his house, and the one that had run him down in New York.

He needed to get closer.

A soft sound came from behind him. A rustle of fabric. A sigh of breath. Spring rain and wildflowers carried on the cold night air. Lacey.

Of course.

"I told you that you were going to be fired if you didn't stay where you were."

"Do you know how many times someone has threatened to fire me?"

"Based on what I've seen so far, a lot."

"Some of my clients fire me ten or twenty times a day."

"Then I guess I've got a ways to go." Jude reached back and grabbed her hand, pulling her up beside him.

"Is the car still there?"

"Yeah."

"Let me see." She squeezed in closer, her hair brushing his chin as she jockeyed for a better position.

Jude pulled her up short. Her wrist was warm beneath his hand. For a moment he was back in the restaurant, Lacey's creamy skin peeking out from under her dark sweater, white scars crisscrossing the tender flesh. She'd shoved her sleeve down too quickly for him to get a good look, but the glimpse he'd gotten was enough. There was a lot more to Lacey than met the eye. A lot she hid behind a quick smile and a quicker wit. She'd been hurt before, and he wouldn't let it happen again. No way was he going to drag her into danger. Not now. Not tomorrow. Not ever. As soon as they got back to the house, he was going to do exactly what he'd threatened—fire her.

"It's not the car." She said it with such authority, Jude stepped from the shadows and took a closer look.

"Why do you say that?"

"The one back at the house had tinted glass. Really dark. With this one, you can see in the back window. Looks like there is a couple sitting in the front seats. Unless you've got two people after you, I don't think that's the same car."

She was right.

Of course she was.

Jude could see inside the car, see the couple in the front seats. If he'd been thinking with his head instead of acting on the anger that had been simmering in his gut for months, he would have seen those things long before now. "You'd make a good detective, Lacey."

"You think so? Maybe I should make a career change. Give up home-care aide for something more dangerous and exciting." She laughed as she pulled away from his hold and stepped out into the parking lot, but there was tension in her shoulders and in the air. As if she sensed the danger that had been stalking Jude, felt it as clearly as Jude did.

"I'm not sure being a detective is as dangerous or as exciting as people think. Most days it's a lot of running into brick walls. Backing up, trying a new direction." He spoke as he led Lacey across the parking lot, his body still humming with adrenaline.

"That sounds like life to me. Running into brick walls, backing up and trying new directions."

"True, but in my job the brick walls happen every other day. In life, they're usually not as frequent." He waited while she got into her car, then closed the door, glancing in the black sedan as he walked past. An elderly woman smiled and waved at him, and Jude waved back, still irritated with himself for the mistake he'd made.

Now that he was closer, it was obvious the two cars

he'd seen weren't the same. The one at his place had been sleeker and a little more sporty. Which proved that when a person wanted to see something badly enough, he did.

"That wasn't much of a meal for you. Sorry to cut things short for a false alarm." He glanced at Lacey as he got into the Mustang, and was surprised that her hand was shaking as she shoved the key into the ignition.

He put a hand on her forearm. "Are you okay?"

"Fine."

"For someone who is fine, your hands sure are shaking hard."

"How about we chalk it up to fatigue?"

"How about you admit you were scared?"

"Were? I still am." She started the car, and Jude let his hand fall away from her arm.

"You don't have to be. We're safe. For now."

"It's the 'for now' part that's got me worried. Who's trying to kill you, Jude? Why?"

"If I had the answers to those questions, we wouldn't be sitting here talking about it."

"You don't even have a suspect?"

"Lacey, I've got a dozen suspects. More. Every wife who's ever watched me cart her husband off to jail. Every son who's ever seen me put handcuffs on his dad. Every family member or friend who's sat through a murder trial and watched his loved one get convicted because of the evidence I put together."

"Have you made a list?"

"I've made a hundred lists. None of them have done me any good. Until the person responsible comes calling again, I've got no evidence, no clues and no way to link anyone to the hit and run."

"Maybe he won't come calling again. Maybe the hit and run was an accident, and maybe the sedan we saw outside your house was just someone who got lost and ended up in the wrong place." She sounded like she really wanted to believe it. He should let her. That's what he'd done with his family. Let them believe the hit and run was a fluke thing that had happened and was over. He'd done it to keep them safe. He'd do the opposite to keep Lacey from getting hurt.

* * * * *

Will Jude manage to scare Lacey away, or will he learn that the best way to keep her safe is to keep her close...for as long as they both shall live? To find out, read
THE DEFENDER'S DUTY by Shirlee McCoy.
Available May 2009
from Love Inspired Suspense.